THE TILLING
SMUGGLERS

The Tilling Smugglers: A Tale of Tilling in
the Style of the Originals by E. F. Benson
Hugh Ashton

ISBN-13: 978-1-912605-78-1

ISBN-10: 1-91-260578-3

Published by j-views Publishing, 2022

© 2022 Hugh Ashton & j-views Publishing

www.HughAshtonBooks.com

www.j-views.biz

publish@j-views.biz

j-views Publishing, 26 Lombard Street, Lichfield, WS13 6DR, UK

CONTENTS

INTRODUCTION

This is the fifth Mapp and Lucia pastiche that I have produced – and it has taken me longer to write it than it took to write the previous stories, for a variety of reasons, partly because it does in fact contain more words, partly because I was simultaneously writing and promoting another book (completely unrelated to Mapp and Lucia), and partly because of personal matters.

This one has been fun to write. Once again, the characters, including the new arrival in Tilling, took over and dictated the plot to me.

I wanted to introduce a character who was professionally involved in the arts, but not the type of aesthete who was encountered by Lucia in her conquest of London. I grew quite fond of Quentin Bontemps as time went on, and there is perhaps an element of wish-fulfilment there – meaning that I would like the ability to pour oil on troubled waters with the same degree of efficiency as him.

I've added a surprising (and some may feel uncanonical) element to Mapp's character – a rather surprising sense of humour. Somehow, I don't feel this is totally unexpected.

Once more, very special thanks to my friend Victoria Yardley, who once again took the trouble to read through what I thought was a print-ready manuscript, and proved me wrong. All remaining misteaks are mine.

And thanks to you and all who have made this series such an unexpected success. It's been a wonderful experience seeing the positive reactions to my work.

So, I bid you *au reservoir*, until the next time.

Hugh Ashton
Lichfield, 2022

THE TILLING SMUGGLERS

A TALE OF TILLING IN THE STYLE OF THE ORIGINALS BY E.F. BENSON

HUGH ASHTON

J-VIEWS PUBLISHING, LICHFIELD, UK

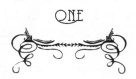

ONE

"Have you seen Major Benjy today?" Diva Plaistow asked Georgie Pillson as he came out of Twistevant's, having ordered some hothouse grapes to be sent to Mallards.

"Good morning," he answered, raising his hat (a new straw boater, with a rather dashing ribbon of purple and salmon pink). "No. In fact I don't think I have laid eyes on him since Sunday at church. Why?"

"Corduroy trousers. Flannel shirt. Carrying spade. Got on tram with it. Extraordinary," Diva replied telegraphically.

"I agree, that does seem rather strange," Georgie replied. "He didn't say anything, I take it?"

"Not a word," Diva said, with an air of regret. "Ho hum. I suppose we'll hear all about it in time. Oh, there's the Padre and Evie. I wonder if they have heard anything."

"Good morrow to ye, Mistress Plaistow, and to you, Master Pillson," the Padre greeted them when he and his wife joined them in answer to Diva's summoning hail. "And what news this fair morn?"

"Major Benjy," said Diva enigmatically.

"Och aye. I ken well what you mean. I saw him wearing a most strange outfit—"

"—just like Irene," squeaked Evie.

"Strange for him, I meant to say. Carrying a spade and fairly running for the tram, I ween. On his way to dig and delve, I dinna doubt."

"But you don't know why?" Georgie asked.

"I was hoping that you might be able to tell me," the Padre said, Scotland seemingly forgotten. "I had the notion that he might have taken up as a navvy."

"I would think that to be most unlikely," said Georgie. "I don't think that Elizabeth would allow that."

"Aye, that's a fair point and a' that. Well, we must be stepping, wee wifie and I. No time to stand gawking with a sermon to write."

"'Gawking' indeed," sniffed Diva when he had gone. "Ha!"

"Here's Elizabeth coming up the street," said Georgie. "We could ask her."

"You're as likely to get sense out of her as you are out of this paving-stone," said Diva. "Anyway, I am not going to be talking to her. She took the last duck at Rice's right from under my nose. She knew I was going to order a duck because I'd told her the day before that I had planned on one, and when I got to Rice's later on he said to me that Mrs Mapp-Flint had just been in and taken the last one. So I'll see you later, Mr Georgie, and do let me know if you find out anything."

Georgie promised to do so, and tipped his hat twice in quick succession, once in farewell to Diva, and once in greeting to Elizabeth Mapp-Flint, who, like Christmas in the month of December, was approaching too rapidly for comfort.

"Was that dear Diva?" Elizabeth asked, knowing full well what the answer would be.

"It was indeed. She remembered that she had left some pastry-fingers in the oven and wanted to get back to Wasters before they burned." Georgie, though usually honest, counted kindness among his virtues, and if telling a lie, even one such as this that was destined for instant disbelief, would prevent friction between his friends and acquaintances, then he was prepared to perpetrate the misdeed. He was about to follow this up with a question about Elizabeth's husband, but she pre-empted him with a transparent falsehood of her own.

"Dear Benjy-boy," she said. "He woke up this morning with the idea that he would go down to the marshes and collect samphire for our dinner tonight. So good with roast duck, you know." She examined Georgie closely to determine if this last would produce any reaction, but Georgie's face remained almost as mute as the paving-stones to which Diva had alluded. A closer observer than Elizabeth (and they would have to be a very close observer indeed) might have noticed a faint twitching of Georgie's moustache, but no more than that showed on his face.

"Indeed?" he said politely. "I am sure that it will be delicious."

"And now," Elizabeth said brightly, "I must be returning to our dear little Grebe. Such a long way from the centre of town, you know, but beggars can't be choosers." This was yet another jab forming part of the collection comprising her long-standing litany of complaints that she had been forced by Lucia's flagrant deception with regards to investments (as she saw it) or by her own short-sightedness and greed (as others saw it) to leave her Queen Anne house in the centre of Tilling, which was now occupied by Lucia and Georgie.

"Stuff and nonsense," said Diva, when Georgie called in at Wasters to tell her about the samphire. "Can you imagine the Major going out and looking for samphire? He wouldn't know it if he saw it. And as for Elizabeth eating the stuff... That would be like seeing pigs flying down the High Street. There's something funny going on there, Mr Georgie, and I am sure we will find out quite soon exactly what it is."

Lucia, when Georgie arrived back at Mallards, was of the same opinion as Diva. "Elizabeth eating a weed that her Benjy-boy has picked by the seaside? I think not. And how very typical of her with regard to poor Diva's duck. We should invite Diva round for dinner and give her a feast some time soon. Poor thing. I fear she is too busy looking after her tea-shop customers to take care of herself."

"Whom should we invite as a companion for her? Irene?"

"I think so," said Lucia, making a note on a notepad, before tearing off the sheet and pinning it to a cork board that stood beside her writing-desk.

Georgie noted that there were many similar notes pinned to the board. "Are those all people whom we must invite to dinner?" he asked.

Lucia gave her silvery laugh in a descending minor key. "Oh no, my dear," she said. "These are little notes to myself. I find myself shockingly forgetful now that I have so many matters to concern me. And, Georgie, I have something to tell you... something quite extraordinary. An extraordinary request. I have been offered the chance to perform one of the most prestigious duties that has ever been requested of me, should I wish to accept it."

"What is it?" he asked, seating himself and preparing for what might well end up being quite a long conversation, verging on a monologue.

"At the end of September, a Royal personage

will be visiting Tilling, and it is envisaged that he – or it may be she – I have not as yet been informed of the identity of the visitor – will be in need of entertainment during the visit. The Mayor has sent me this letter," waving an envelope with the arms of Tilling embossed on it, "and in it has asked me, given the success of the Elizabethan fête at Riseholme before we moved here, if I would be willing to take the lead in organising such an entertainment."

Georgie, whose feet still ached when he remembered the agony of the shoes he had worn as Sir Francis Drake, winced. "If you are going to produce the Elizabethan fête again, you must find another Francis Drake."

Lucia smiled. "I had no intention of doing so. I had in mind a subject more connected with the history of Tilling than Good Queen Bess."

"What is it to be?" asked Georgie.

Lucia lowered her voice, leaned forward, and whispered in melodramatic tones a single word. Indeed, so melodramatic were the tones that Georgie was unfortunately unable to catch the word.

"I'm sorry, you'll have to speak up," he said.

Lucia sighed. "Smugglers," she said in her usual voice. "Just imagine it," she said. "Bales of French brandy and barrels of silk – or perhaps that should be the other way round, now I come to think of it. Bands of desperate men making their way by moonlight across the marshes to the entrance of their secret tunnel to the Traders Arms. And then the King's Excisemen, waiting patiently with dark-lanterns and drawn pistols. And the final courtroom scene with the judge finally donning the black cap as the wretched miscreants are condemned to be hanged."

"I see," said Georgie, wondering how such a spectacle could be staged at night.

"Of course, we will need lots of actors to take the various roles, and I will need all the support I can find if I am to make a success of this. Without you behind me, my dear, there is no possible way I can undertake this. So I entreat you to provide me with the support I will need to turn my ideas into a production worthy of the attention of the Royal personage. I can then assure the Mayor and the Corporation that they will not be disappointed in their choice of me as the director of this event."

Georgie knew full well that whatever he said at this point, Lucia would go ahead, with or without his support. "Of course," he sighed.

"Very well," said Lucia brightly. "The first thing we must do is to find our cast."

"Wouldn't it be better to work out the script first, so that we know what characters we will need to cast?"

Lucia considered this for a moment. "Do you know, Georgie, I think you may be right there. Dear me, this might be quite difficult. I am certainly going to need your assistance."

"Will there be speaking parts, or will you be presenting it as a series of tableaux?"

"I had been thinking of it being presented in much the same way as our little Riseholme Elizabethan triumph. Most of the parts will be silent, but there will be a few speeches from the major characters – the leader of the smugglers, the chief of the Excisemen, and of course the judge in the final scene."

Georgie began to laugh quietly.

"What is so amusing?" Lucia asked him.

"I think you might ask Major Benjy to be the chief of the smugglers' band. I think he would be perfect in that role, don't you?"

"Oo is vewy naughty boy to say such things," Lucia told him, but she herself was now laughing. "But you are perfectly right. He would make an excellent smuggler chief."

"And the head of the Excisemen would be Mr Wyse?"

"You are inspired today, Georgie."

"And for the judge..." Georgie ventured, hoping that Lucia would take the hint and nominate him for the part.

"Since there is to be a judge, I feel I should take that part. After all, I have been a magistrate for some years now, and I know how a court of law should be conducted. I shall make a speech – not too long, somewhere in the region of five or ten minutes – in which I shall condemn the smugglers' trade, and emphasise the loyalty of Tilling to the King and to his ministers."

"And for me?"

"For you, perhaps the wicked landlord of the inn where the smugglers hide their loot. Yes, I see it now, with Diva as your wife, who also plays a role as barmaid and serving girl."

"I see. An innkeeper," said Georgie, and there was more than a hint of bitterness in his voice.

"But it is a most important part of the story," Lucia protested, "and in any case, since we are writing this little piece, we can give you a very good part. Perhaps you can betray the smugglers to the Excisemen? Yes..." Her face took on a dreamy look as she gazed, seemingly at the scene in her imagination. "I can see it now. Let us write this down before we forget."

Several sheets of foolscap later, Lucia felt herself satisfied with the progress so far.

"What are we going to do," Georgie asked, as a thought struck him, "about Elizabeth? Can we invite Major Benjy to take a part, and not Elizabeth? And Susan Wyse, for that matter?"

"We should have a female chorus to sing sea-shanties," Lucia told him. "Evie can direct it, and Diva and Elizabeth can join her."

"Can women sing sea-shanties? I thought it was meant to be bad luck or something. Or is it whistling at sea that brings bad luck?"

"I'm sure I don't know," said Lucia. "But I am sure I have some music for shanties somewhere. Let us search for it."

THREE

Elizabeth sat in the dining-room, waiting for her husband to return from wherever it was that he had gone that morning, wearing his oldest clothes and bearing a spade over his shoulder as if he were carrying a gun.

When she had asked him where he was going, he had merely tapped the side of his nose in that irritating fashion of his, and said, "Mum's the word, old girl, but you'll have a wonderful surprise soon, believe me." Since then, it was clear that he had been observed by quite a number of Tillingites, and she had been forced to invent that ridiculous story about samphire in order to cover her (or rather her husband's) tracks.

It was now past two o'clock, and she was hungry. Just as she had decided that it was pointless to wait any longer, and was about to ring the bell for Withers to bring in the cottage pie (now, she feared, dried out to inedible crumbs) she heard the kitchen door open and shut, and the sound of Withers greeting Major Mapp-Flint as the prodigal returned.

He stood in the doorway a minute or two later, in stockinged feet, and with his hands ostentatiously washed. His trousers and jacket were noticeably muddy, however.

"Where have you been?" asked Elizabeth, horrified. "I cannot and shall not wait any longer for luncheon. I shall start my food, and I suggest that you go upstairs and change your clothes. I am not going to have you sitting down at the table in that state."

Rather than his being annoyed at these orders, which he had expected, the Major took them in good part. "Very well, Liz," he smiled. "But just wait until you hear what I have to tell you."

Elizabeth had just finished her dried-up cottage pie and watery cabbage when Benjy came down in high good humour.

"Jolly good morning's work," he smiled at her. "You're in for the treat of your life, my girl." He looked down at the plate that Withers had just placed in front of him and laughed. "I said to myself as I was coming down the stairs that I was so hungry that I could eat a horse. Well, it looks as though this was a horse in its younger days, and very glad I am to be eating it."

It was quite unlike the Major to be so cavalier about his food. Usually if the meals served to him were not to his liking he would complain, though he had learned by bitter experience not to do this too vociferously within Elizabeth's hearing.

Rather than address the origin of the meat contained in the cottage pie, which while not being horsemeat, was nonetheless the cheapest cut of lamb that Elizabeth had managed to extract from the butcher, she asked the obvious question. The dam of reticence that forms a part of human nature, even Elizabeth's, was incapable of withstanding the pressure of the curiosity building up inside her.

"What on earth have you been doing with yourself all morning, Benjy-boy?" she asked.

"Aha!" he exclaimed. "What if I were to tell you it was a secret?"

"And what if I was to tell you that there should be no such secrets between husband and wife?"

"Quite right, Liz," he said. "But what I'm about to tell you is a secret that stays between this husband and this wife. I believe we are soon to become very wealthy."

Elizabeth eyed him suspiciously. "I trust you have not been taking advice from Lucia on stocks and shares," she said.

"Nothing like that." He dropped his voice to a conspiratorial whisper. "I'm taking about buried treasure."

Elizabeth choked on her marmalade sponge pudding. "Buried treasure?" she scoffed. "Is that why you went out with that spade over your shoulder this morning?" Benjy nodded. "And where, exactly do you think you will find buried treasure here in Tilling? What on earth could have given you that idea?"

"Captain Puffin," mumbled her husband.

"Did you say 'Captain Puffin'?" she asked indignantly. The memory of the late Captain still had the power to arouse a passionate storm. Before he had so imaginatively drowned in a plate of oxtail soup one Christmas Day some years past, he and Major Flint (as he had been known before his marriage to Elizabeth) had been regular partners at golf and at nightly debauches (for so Elizabeth considered their evenings together) at which quantities of whisky were consumed. After one of these evenings, Puffin, intoxicated himself, had accused Elizabeth of drunkenness. The resulting outrage that Elizabeth had displayed had led to the Major, by some sort of psychic *jujitsu* which still remained inexplicable to him, taking her side against the Captain's, and eventually combining her name with his, rather than her becoming Mrs Mapp-Puffin. It might be stretching a point to refer to the Major and the Captain as having been friends, but it was certainly true to claim that they had enjoyed their disputes with each other, whether occasioned by golf or by whisky, more than they would have enjoyed them with anyone else.

"Indeed, I did mention his name, God rest his soul," he replied. "One day he told me that he believed that he had discovered the site of treasure that had been buried more than one hundred years ago."

"Ridiculous!" Elizabeth scoffed. "Why has no one else discovered it? And, pray, why did he not dig it up and take it for himself, if indeed it ever existed? My feeling is that it was a dream caused by an excess of whisky."

"Just so, Liz, just so," replied the Major equably. He had now finished his cottage pie, and was starting on his marmalade sponge pudding. "Exactly what I said to Puffin when he told me. He said that it had been buried in the sand-dunes, and that one day when he was walking, he saw the corner of a box which had been exposed by the sand. He didn't have any spade or tools with him, of course, but he managed to remove some of the sand, and he saw that the box was an antique chest, with what looked like barrels beside it. It was far too much for him to carry on his own, so he decided to tell me about it. We were due to go and collect the box from there the week after that Christmas. We thought it would be the perfect time – everyone full of Christmas and not going out. And then, of course, poor old Puffin went and died."

By now, Elizabeth was intrigued. "One sand-dune looks very much like another," she said. "How would he know where to look again?"

"Ah, this is where the Navy showed its true stuff," said the Major. "Since he had been a sailor, Puffin always carried a compass with him, and he worked out what he called 'the bearings' of Tilling church tower, and other landmarks. Before he died, he gave me a piece of paper with these bearings, and I used it today to find the box."

"So you did find it?"

"Indeed I did," he said, wiping his moustache with his napkin. "Too heavy for me to lift. No wonder a little shrimp like Puffin found it impossible to move. And there is more besides. Barrels, my dear Liz, barrels full of the finest French brandy."

"How would they come to be there?"

"Smugglers. This was a cache, hidden by a smuggler in the hope that one day he would come back and retrieve it. And perhaps he drowned at sea, or the long arm of the law caught him. In any case, the barrels and the box are indeed there, just as Puffin told me."

"And what is in that box?"

"We will discover that together."

Elizabeth felt a glow of excitement run through her veins. She had long since abandoned the idea of stormy romance sweeping her off her feet. Whatever other qualities Major Benjy might possess, a high degree of romantic feeling would be one of the last that any acquaintance of his could ascribe to him. However, the idea of buried treasure, and a box which might contain – what? Gold, silver, jewels? Possibly not, as she brought her thoughts down to earth. But what else did smugglers smuggle? Tobacco, she recalled. Well, Major Benjy was welcome to that, as long as he didn't smoke it indoors. But silk was another form of contraband, she seemed to remember. What if (and here her imagination started to take wing and rise towards the empyrean) the box contained yards and yards of the most delicious silk, which could be made up into the most stunning garments with which to dazzle Tilling?

Miss Greele, her usual dressmaker, would probably lack the experience to make up garments from such a fabric, and it might be necessary to go to Worthing or Hastings, or even Brighton, in order to find a workman (or workwoman) worthy of his (or her) hire, but what was that compared to the weeping and wailing and gnashing of teeth that would ensue when she first wore the luxurious garment that was even now taking final shape in her imagination?

Susan Wyse's sables, the skins of some poor dead animals, would pale in comparison (she forced herself not to dwell on the origins of silk), and as for Lucia...

She smiled at Benjy. "When can we start?"

FOUR

Lucia and Georgie were busy planning the Smuggler's Pageant. They had suggested various names for the event to each other, but none of them had met with unanimous approval, and so "The Smuggler's Pageant" it was, until such time as further inspiration should strike. Even then, there was a slight difference of opinion, with Georgie contending that the apostrophe should come after the last letter of "Smugglers", since there was to be more than one smuggler taking part, but Lucia had it in mind to focus on the leader of the gang, and therefore she believed a singular apostrophe to be more appropriate.

The process of creation could be roughly summarised as follows.

Firstly, Lucia would describe a scene which, while gorgeous and with effects that would amaze and dazzle with their brilliance, would nonetheless be beyond the technical capabilities of even the most sophisticated London West End theatres to produce.

Secondly, Georgie would gently but firmly point out the practicalities which would accompany the staging of such a scene.

"Yes, I agree that a broadside of cannon fired from a Customs sloop" (Lucia had been looking up various nautical terms and had been particularly taken with some of them) "would be extremely effective. However, I do not know if we can find twenty cannon in time, let alone the crews to man and fire them. Or the gunpowder for that matter, even if it's allowed, which I doubt. And then," he pointed out, "the noise would be hidjus. If we were to rehearse this, my nerves would be in shreds by the time the performance came around. And the cows would stop laying eggs, and the hens would stop giving milk – you know what I mean – and everyone would blame you."

Thirdly, Lucia would attempt a compromise.

Lucia furrowed her brow. "I see what you

mean, Georgie. Perhaps one small cannon, then."

Fourthly, Georgie would make another objection, this time on the grounds of artistic licence.

"But that wouldn't be very real. You can't imagine a gang of desperate smugglers running away or surrendering from just one small cannon."

Fifthly and finally, Lucia would put the idea to one side for an indefinite period.

"Oh, very well, Georgie. But let us consider it in the future."

And that was the end of the cannon broadside.

After borrowing several tales of swashbuckling adventure from the library, Georgie proved himself to be quite adept at writing in what Lucia termed an "antique nautical style" which was full of lines such as "Avast, me hearties", and "Belay that, my brave lads".

"I don't know who Davy Jones was," Georgie said to Lucia, "or why he had a locker, but it seems that it was a popular place to send people in those days."

"Strange," agreed Lucia. "You would have thought he would be in the *National Dictionary of Biography*, would you not? But your words for the smuggler chief and the captain of the

Excisemen really do bring the romance of the ocean onto dry land. I can almost taste the salt spray and hear the sound of the wind in the rigging as I read them."

"I think you had better write the court scenes, though," said Georgie. "I don't know anything about the law, except that you're meant to have a lamp on your bicycle when you go out at night – or is it two lamps? Anyway, I'm sure I'd make a mess of it, and when the Royal personage comes, they are bound to know everything about the law, because it's their job and they'd just laugh at my ignorance, and that would be horrid."

"Very well, my dear. Remember, I am still a Justice of the Peace, and of course," her voice trembled a little, "Pepino was called to the Bar."

"I *am* sorry," said Georgie. "I had no intention of reviving painful memories."

"Of course you didn't," said Lucia. "Please don't trouble yourself about it. Now," and she brightened. "Do you think that we could ask the Padre if the Boy Scouts would like to be smugglers?"

"He might find it rather strange for us to be asking that," said Georgie. "Aren't Boy Scouts meant to be doing good deeds, and not breaking the law? I don't think the Padre would approve, do you? They might be Customs men, though."

Lucia sighed. "I suppose you're right. Though of course they'd only be pretending. We're not asking them to actually be smugglers, just to pretend to be smugglers."

"Then let's ask the Padre and see what he says," Georgie said. "I think you'd better ask him. I feel he will certainly listen to what you have to say."

"I think it is a man's job. I really do believe that you are so very much better at these things than I am."

"Oh, very well then. I shall make a memorandum in my book," said Georgie, and did so, reflecting that Lucia most likely did not want to suffer the indignity of the almost certain refusal of the request.

FIVE

Major Mapp-Flint was more than a little surprised by his wife's enthusiasm for the hidden smuggler's hoard, but decided to strike while the iron was hot.

"Then we'll go there this afternoon," he told her. "We will see what we will see."

Accordingly, Elizabeth went upstairs to put on her oldest gardening clothes, and once she was changed, presented herself for Benjy's inspection.

"Just the ticket, old girl," he said. "Grab yourself a spade or something from the garden shed, and off we go."

The small procession of two set off for the sand-dunes. Happily, they met no one, otherwise Elizabeth would have had to expand on the story of samphire to a degree where even the most credulous would find it hard to believe that such a passion for the vegetable had developed at Grebe that it was necessary for two foragers to supply the needs of the household.

Benjy removed a compass from his pocket, and sighted along it until he was satisfied, and then set off at an oblique angle across the dunes, keeping an eye on the compass all the way.

Elizabeth scrambled after him, the sand seeping over the top of her shoes and resting uncomfortably in the toes. There were strange grey insects scurrying over the surface of the sand, and she was convinced that at least one of them had jumped onto her ankle, and was even now scaling the Everest of her leg, but she dared not look too closely.

At length her husband called a halt. "Somewhere here," he said. "Cast your eye about and look for the corner of a box."

It was Elizabeth who discovered it, and proudly pointed it out to Benjy.

"Well done, Liz," he said. "That's it, all right. Now, let's have a look at it." He attacked the sand around the protruding corner of the box with his spade, and Elizabeth assisted by using her hoe to remove some of the sand where she guessed the rest of the box might be hiding.

"It certainly is big," she admitted, when the majority of the box lay exposed. It was the size of a large steamer trunk, bound with brass, now tarnished, and fastened with three strong metal hasps and padlocks. The Major took hold of one of the handles at one end, and heaved until the veins stood out on his forehead, and his face turned an alarming shade of bright red.

"Lend a hand, Liz," he requested, but even with their combined efforts, the box proved impossible to move more than a few inches.

"Can't we open it?" Elizabeth asked.

"I'll need to get some tools from somewhere to get those locks off," pointed out the Major.

"Perhaps you might be able to remove them with the spade?"

"I'll give it a shot. Stand back," he warned her. After three hefty blows with the spade, the first padlock and hasp fell off.

"Oh well done," Elizabeth encouraged him. "Splendid work."

The glow that spread over Major Benjy's face was not merely the result of exertion, but of pride at his success being recognised in this way.

"Now for the next one," he said, and swung his spade at it. This time it took a few more blows before the lock and hasp flew off.

"Whew," he panted. "Time for a quick breather." He reached for his hip pocket, but stopped his hand when it was halfway there, covering his move with a dive into his trouser pocket from which he extracted a large handkerchief with which he mopped his face.

"Here we go," he said after a few minutes, taking up the spade again. This time it took only two blows before the padlock flew off.

"Well done, my Benjy-boy," Elizabeth congratulated him.

With a "one, two, three," from the Major, they opened the lid of the chest together. A strong smell of tobacco filled their nostrils, and Elizabeth started to sneeze violently.

"There's some stuff in here," Benjy said to her. "Just take a look at this." He held up a length of royal blue silk. "All different colours."

Elizabeth saw for herself. An Aladdin's cave of silk – enough to keep the dressmakers of Hastings busy for months. She could imagine herself in a different outfit every day of the year – gorgeous, floating dresses, all made of the purest antique silk. And... "There might be enough here to make you a waistcoat or two," she said to Benjy. "Competition for Mr Georgie."

"Hah!" he exclaimed. "That would be a turn up for the books, wouldn't it? To out-milliner Miss Milliner Michael-Angelo. Thirsty work this," and this time he quite openly reached for his hip flask and took a swig of the contents.

"Benjy-boy!" she scolded him, but she took care not to crack the whip too hard, since she was well aware that she would need his assistance in order to move the silk – there was far too much for her to carry away by herself.

"Sorry, old girl. Needed that," he answered. "But we haven't come to what I think is the best part."

It was hard for Elizabeth to imagine what could possibly be regarded as better than yard after yard of the finest antique silks and brocades, but she watched with interest as her husband scratched around in the sand, and revealed what appeared to be the top of a small barrel.

"Those smugglers didn't just bring in silk from France," he said with an air of satisfaction. "Brandy, my girl. And this is over one hundred years old. Do you know what this would be worth if it were bottled? It could fetch as much as twenty-five pounds a bottle, or perhaps even more."

Despite herself, Elizabeth was impressed. Though she knew next to nothing about vintage cognac from the time of Napoleon, she was well aware of the value of twenty-five pounds, and what that might mean.

"The problem is," she said, "that we can't risk bringing any of this back to Grebe in the daylight in case we're seen."

"Would it matter?" he asked.

"Oh dear," Elizabeth said. "I really shouldn't have to explain all this to you. First of all, you tell me that this is a smuggler's hoard?"

"Yes."

"Which means that all of this, this silk and the brandy, is here without anyone having paid duty on it. It's contraband, Benjy, and we could be thrown into prison if we are found with it."

"Rubbish," the Major retorted. "Stuff and nonsense. This was left here over a hundred years ago. Finders keepers, my girl. They can't touch us."

"I wouldn't be so sure about that. Lucia is still a Justice of the Peace, and I am sure that she'd welcome any chance to make trouble. Even though she stopped being Mayor some years ago, she still talks about 'my Inspector'." Here

Elizabeth made a rude noise. "Her Inspector indeed! But that's the way she thinks, and we must be on our guard. Once all of this is in the house, of course, we can make up any story we like about it, and who can say nay to us? But if we're found carrying it from the beach to Grebe..."

"I begin to see what you're saying. Is there any more?"

"Of course there is. If we are seen carrying this, people will wonder where it has come from, and they will start looking. And then everyone will take it for themselves before we have removed it to Grebe."

Her husband stroked his moustache thoughtfully. "By Jove, you have worked it out most wonderfully, Liz. What do you propose that we do, then?"

"We must work by night. And we must use the gardener's wheelbarrow to convey the silks and the brandy – and who knows what else there might be – as efficiently as possible."

Benjy, whose back was already aching in anticipation of pushing a heavily laden wheelbarrow across the sand-dunes, groaned his agreement.

"And now," continued Elizabeth, "we must

cover over what we have discovered, and go back ready to make our move this evening."

At Mallards, Georgie and Lucia were still wrestling with the plot and casting of the pageant. Lucia had deputed Georgie to ask the Padre if the Boy Scouts could be recruited as smugglers.

"It needs a man's firm hand to persuade him," she had said, but Georgie was unconvinced that his hands, though those of a man, would be firm enough on this occasion.

However, he made his way to the Vicarage, and was admitted to wait in the room used as a study, while the Padre finished a telephone call.

The room may have been named a "study", thought Georgie to himself, but there were remarkably few books on the shelves, the majority appearing to be books of nineteenth-century sermons which could be picked up by the yard from auction houses, and the desk at which the Padre presumably composed his own sermons appeared to be remarkably free of encumbrances such as paper, pens or ink.

At length, the Padre came in.

"I was just talking to the Bishop," he said, in what was neither Scotch nor medieval English. Presumably he dispensed with such luxuries when conversing with his spiritual superiors, and had forgotten to resume them. "He tells me that he will be delighted to attend the festivities surrounding the visit of the Royal personage to Tilling and has very graciously agreed to give the blessing at the special service to be held that day."

"How very gratifying," said Georgie. "It is exactly about these festivities that I have come to see you."

"Och, weel," said the Padre, his speech migrating over the Border once more. "And how may I be helping ye, Maister Pillson?"

"Well, there's going to be a pageant," began Georgie.

"Aye, I had heard something aboot that," said

the Padre. "'Twill concern pirates and buccaneers, and the like, I hear tell."

"Not quite," Georgie corrected him.
"Smugglers, not pirates. And I'm not sure of
the difference between pirates and buccaneers, but I'm sure we don't have any of them
planned."

"Aye, pirates, buccaneers, smugglers. All of
them evildoers and sinners in the sight of the
Lord."

"Then I suppose I would be wasting my time
if I were to ask you if the Boy Scouts could
take part as a band of smugglers?"

Despite the earlier words of condemnation,
it was clear to Georgie that the Padre was se-
riously considering the possibility. With what
Georgie later described to Lucia as a brilliant
flash of inspiration, he added, "And of course,
you would be the captain – the leader of the
band of smugglers. A brace of pistols stuck in
your belt, a cutlass at your side..." He paused
to allow the Padre to consider the splendours
of the costume.

"Aye, weel, it may be that we could consider
it. I dinna consider it reet and proper, though,
that a man of the cloth, such as myself, should
take on such a part. Could ye not decide that

they will be the Excise, though, with myself at their head?"

This was, after all, an option that Georgie and Lucia had previously discussed, and Georgie admitted to the Padre that this might indeed be a possibility. "I think that might be more suitable, yes," he said. "But we will still need smugglers. Where are we to find them, do you think?"

"Begorrah, to be sure there's a problem that you have there," said the Padre, his speech crossing the Irish Sea in a single unexpected bound. "I dinna ken of such folk around here," he continued, returning to the British mainland as quickly as he had left it.

"I had heard," suggested Georgie, "that there used to be smugglers in these parts. Perhaps their descendants still live here, and might be interested?"

"Och aye, but that was many years ago, and I dinna suppose that they would be rightly pleased to be reminded of the deeds of their great-grandpas."

Georgie was forced to return to Lucia with the news that he had failed to recruit a band of smugglers, but had at least secured the Excisemen.

"Then we will have to cast our net wider

afield," said Lucia. "We must not despair." She paused, and looked her husband full in the face. "Georgie, you shall be the leader of the smugglers."

He recoiled with a look of terror on his face. "No, no, I couldn't possibly do that," he said. "I mean, I just couldn't..." His voice tailed off, and he sank, seemingly overcome, into his seat. "Totally out of the question," he said with a little more firmness. "Totally. And that is my last word."

"Well then," said Lucia. "I had no idea that you were going to be so difficult about this."

"I am not being difficult," Georgie said. "You know perfectly well that I detest going on stage, even when it's for our tableaux in front of friends, and it's simply impossible for me to take such a large part if there's going to be a Royal Personage watching. Why, even the thought of it has made me feel all faint. Being an innkeeper is quite enough for me, and I am not sure that I can even manage that."

"Oo poor widdle Georgie," said Lucia, lapsing into their private language. "*Poverino*. Naughty Lucia to think of such a thing."

"Quite. But it does leave us with a problem, I do understand that." He sat, fanning his face with his handkerchief. "Irene!" he exclaimed suddenly.

"The quaint one? What about her?"

"She is to be the leader of the smugglers, of course. Who better?"

"But she's—" Lucia broke off, unable to frame her thought with the delicacy she felt it deserved.

"You mean she's not a man," said Georgie. "That's true, but not so that you would notice most of the time. And her maid Lucy will make a wonderful second-in-command, dressed up properly."

A dreamy look came over Lucia's face as she appeared to consider the prospect. "I see it now," she said. "Irene clad in knee-breeches, a cutlass in her hand, a bottle of rum in the other, pistols in her belt, a patch over one eye... Yes, my dear, I think you have hit on the answer."

"I believe you are thinking of pirates, rather than smugglers," Georgie told her. "But I'm glad you agree with my suggestion. I'll go and talk to her about it."

"If anyone can get her to agree to her taking part, it will be you," Lucia told him.

SEVEN

Once Georgie had arrived at Taormina, and seated himself carefully in a chair (after a preliminary minute inspection to ensure that no stray specks of paint would sully the pristine nature of his new trousers), he started to explain the scheme and the lack of a leader of the gang of smugglers.

"So you see, the Padre's refused, Lucia is not talking to Elizabeth, after the time Elizabeth was caught revoking at the Wyses' bridge evening the other week and refused to admit it, even though everyone could see that she had. So what that means is we can't ask Major Benjy—"

"He'd be good, though," Irene interrupted.

"He's got just the kind of rogue's face that would pass as a smuggler."

"Yes, he would look good," Georgie agreed, "I'm not sure that we should tell him that his face is that roguish, though. Anyway, it's out of the question right now. And I believe the Wyses will be in Capri for a lot of the time between now and then, which means that they won't be able to come to rehearsals. So that leaves..."

"Diva?" suggested Irene, laughing.

Despite himself, Georgie joined in with the laughter. "Irene, that's very naughty of you. How could you possibly imagine such a thing?"

"I'm an artist," she replied simply. "Imagination is my trade."

"Well, then. How do you imagine yourself as the leader of a band of smugglers?"

Irene's face broke into a broad smile. "That's simply the best thing I've heard in ages," she said. "Tell me, was that Lucia's idea or yours?"

Georgie felt himself blushing. "Mine," he admitted.

"You're a dear," Irene told him. "I'd kiss you, except that you'd blush terribly, and I wouldn't want to embarrass you. At least, not so much as that."

"Then you'll do it?" he asked, expectantly.

"Of course I will. How could you doubt it? One thing, though..."

Georgie's heart sank. "What is it?" he asked, nervously.

"Could Lucy be in the pageant as well? As a sort of second in command or something? Or just as one of the smugglers?"

"Oh, is that all?" Georgie sighed with relief. "Of course she can. In fact, I was rather hoping that you would agree to that if I asked you."

"Then that's settled, isn't it?"

"We're going to need more than two smugglers, though. Where are we going to find them?"

"Will you trust me to find your smugglers?" Irene asked. "How many do you need?"

"Not more than a dozen or so, I suppose, not including you and Lucy."

"That should be easy," Irene said with satisfaction. "Trust me. I know just the smugglers you need. Costumes?"

"I'm afraid we haven't really decided on that. But I'll tell you," Georgie went on as a happy thought struck him. "Why don't you and I decide on costumes together? Your artistic skills and eye..."

"...and your exquisite taste— No, my dear, I'm

not mocking you. You are definitely the best-dressed man in Tilling."

Not for the first time, Georgie found himself blushing at Irene's words, despite her earlier protestation. "M–most kind of you to say so," he stammered.

"Not at all. It's nothing but the truth," Irene told him. "Now, when is all this meant to be taking place?"

"Towards the end of September."

"No, no, I mean what period is this all set in? When is it meant to be happening?"

"I'm not exactly sure, but about the time of Napoleon, I suppose."

"I'm sure I've got a book somewhere with pictures," Irene told him. "Come and see me tomorrow. I should have found it by then, and we can look through it together."

EIGHT

True to her word, when Georgie visited her the next day, Irene had retrieved her book of costumes.

Georgie seated himself beside her at the table, and they pored over the pictures in the book together.

"These look rather wonderful," said Georgie, pointing to a picture of gentlemen in knee-breeches and brocaded coats.

"Not for smugglers, though," Irene pointed out. "Not very practical in a boat. Anyway, what are you going to be in this pageant of Lucia's?"

"She said I could be the innkeeper," Georgie admitted. "I didn't really want to be just an innkeeper, since it's not really a very important part of the story. I'd much rather be a smuggler."

"And a very handsome one you would be too, my dear," said Irene. "Your beard is a perfect smuggler's beard. But let's be honest, shall we? I don't think you're nearly wicked enough to be a smuggler."

"I'm sure you mean that as a compliment."

"Of course it's a compliment. But an innkeeper... Let's see. We don't want you in a greasy apron, do we?"

"Certainly not!" said Georgie, indignantly.

"What about this?" suggested Irene, pointing to another plate.

Georgie considered it. "With perhaps a feather in the hat?" he suggested.

"A feather would be perfect."

"But what about you? There don't seem to be any pictures of smugglers in this book."

"I'm sure Lucy and I can manage, don't you worry. And who, may I ask, will be the head of the Excisemen?"

"We had thought of asking Mr Wyse—"

"Oh no, surely not?"

"But he will be away visiting the Contessa, I believe. So we've asked the Padre, and he will lead a troop of Boy Scouts as the Customs officers."

Irene burst into peals of laughter. "Hoots, mon, 'twill be a bonny sight." She paused. "But what about Major Benjy? I know you said that Lucia and Mapp aren't talking to each other, but it does seem a shame to waste that moustache of his."

"He has just the kind of face, too," Georgie said wistfully.

Irene put her head on one side, pensively. "If I could persuade old Benjy-Wenjy to take part, I'd be happy to be an ordinary smuggler."

"And Lucy?"

"She'd be content, too."

"I don't know how you'd manage that, though. Elizabeth would hate you for stealing Benjy from her. At least, that's the way she'd see it."

"She hates me anyway, so there'd be nothing new there. Anyway, it would be fun. And I already have an idea of how to do it."

"How?" he asked curiously.

"Wait and see," was the only answer he could get.

Two days later, Diva was talking to Georgie outside Twistevant's.

"Most mysterious," were the words with which she opened the conversation.

"What is mysterious?" Georgie asked politely.

"Elizabeth and Benjy," Diva said, dropping her voice. "Now you tell me, Mr Georgie, if you can understand what's going on here. Last night I was coming back from Ashford, where I'd been to get a bit of— well, never mind what it was. And I came back in the bus that they run of a summer evening from Ashford to Tilling, and it goes along the road past Grebe. And I saw the two of them walking along the road."

"Well, that doesn't really sound like anything special."

"Ah," Diva said, becoming conspiratorial. "But what were they carrying, and what was with them?"

"I'm sure I don't know," said Georgie, almost crossly. "How can I know if you don't tell me?"

"Well, Major Benjy was pushing a wheelbarrow which seemed to have a spade and a rake in it, from what I could make out, and he and Elizabeth were dressed in some of the oldest and shabbiest clothes I've ever seen either of them wear."

Georgie considered several additions to this last sentence, but decided not to say any of them. "And then?" was what he eventually did come out with.

"I couldn't see," Diva said. "The bus was going too fast and I lost sight of them."

"Well, Elizabeth said the other day that Major Benjy was going to the marshes to pick samphire. She said that it goes well with roast duck."

"The impertinence!" said Diva, memories of stolen ducks still fresh in her mind. "I ask you! Anyway, samphire indeed! She wouldn't know what to do with samphire if you stuffed it up her nose! I'll give you five shillings if any samphire has ever entered her kitchen. Anyway, what do you think they were up to with that wheelbarrow and those tools?"

"I have no idea," Georgie confessed.

"Nor I," said Diva. "I ask you, why would anyone go out at that time of the evening?"

"What time was that?"

"Just a little before half-past six, because the church clock was striking half-past when I walked back home from the bus, and it doesn't take more than ten minutes from Grebe to there on the bus, the way they drive these days."

"Well..." Georgie said. "They're not going to play golf, are they? Not with a hoe and a shovel and a wheelbarrow. I really can't think of anything except gardening."

"Smugglers!" exclaimed Diva suddenly.

Georgie started. "Has Lucia said anything to you?" he enquired.

"About smugglers? No. Why should she?"

Georgie was now on the horns of a dilemma. If he were to tell Diva about the plans for the pageant, she was sure to ask what sort of role she would be expected to play and, since no role had as yet been assigned to her, it might be embarrassing to tell her about it. On the other hand...

"Oh, about the pageant."

"What pageant?"

"Well, this is a bit of a secret, and you really shouldn't repeat it to anyone," Georgie told her, knowing full well that the news would be all over Tilling within a couple of days, and that Elizabeth Mapp-Flint, when she heard about it, would be gnashing her beautiful teeth at the thought of not having been the first to hear of it.

"Well, we'd better go inside in case anyone overhears," said Diva. "Do you like fish-paste?"

"In moderation," said Georgie cautiously. "Why?"

"I've been trying out a new recipe for bloater-paste for sandwiches, and I want another opinion on it," Diva told him. "I think my customers will like it, but I'm not sure."

They made their way to Wasters, and Diva called to Janet to bring a pot of tea and some of the bloater-paste and some bread and butter.

"Well?" she said, leaning forward conspiratorially as they waited.

"We're going to have royalty visiting Tilling," Georgie told her.

"Oh. Who?" Diva asked, trying her best to appear unimpressed by the idea of a Royal visit, but visibly failing in this aim.

"I'm afraid I don't know," Georgie admitted. "Lucia told me about it—"

"—And she wouldn't tell you?" Diva interrupted. "Well, I do call that mean of her. I mean, I'm sorry I said that, because you are married to her, after all, but..." By now, Diva was covered with embarrassment, which Georgie was too gentlemanly to remark on.

"No, I was going to say that she didn't tell me, because she didn't know herself. She was told by the Mayor that this was going to happen, but the Mayor didn't tell her."

"Maybe the Mayor didn't know himself?" suggested Diva, recovering her composure.

The tea and the makings of the bloater-paste sandwiches arrived.

"May I make a suggestion?" Georgie offered, after he had sampled the first sandwich.

"Of course."

"A little horseradish and a few drops of lemon juice added to the mixture might add a little to the taste, and perhaps take away a little of the oiliness of the fish?"

"What a good idea, and how clever you are, Mr Georgie. Now, the Royal visit. Why did the Mayor tell Lucia about it?"

"Do you remember when Lucia and I first

came to Tilling, when we rented Mallards from Elizabeth?"

"I do indeed," Diva remarked stiffly. "Garden-produce and everything," referring to the arrangement that had been made with Lucia, and that which had been made with Diva, with the result that Elizabeth had the use of the garden-produce from both Mallards and Wasters.

"Well, that's all in the past now," Georgie said hurriedly, before Diva could launch into an exposition of the wrongs, real and imaginary, that had been inflicted on her by Elizabeth. "What I was going to say was that Lucia had organised an Elizabethan pageant at Riseholme, where she was the Queen, and I played Sir Francis Drake."

"I remember," said Diva. "It was in the newspapers, wasn't it?"

"That's right, I remember now that it was in the papers," said Georgie, whose scrapbook of press cuttings, including photographs of him as Sir Francis, complete with agonising satin shoes, formed one of his most prized, if secretive, possessions. "Anyway, the Mayor has asked Lucia to produce a pageant for the Royal visit?"

"Elizabeth? The Queen, I mean. Not Elizabeth Mapp-Flint."

"No, it should be connected with Tilling, so it's going to be smugglers."

"How exciting!" Diva exclaimed. "And what are you going to be?"

"Well, Lucia's asked me to take the part of the landlord of the inn where the smugglers used to bring their contraband. You know, silks and brandy and tobacco, and so on. There was a secret passage, you know, which led from the Traders Arms to the next street, which the smugglers would use when the Customs men came searching for them."

"And Lucia? Will she be leading the smugglers?"

"No, she felt that it would set a bad example as a former Mayor and a magistrate to be seen leading a group of criminals, even if it was just for a pageant. She wants to be the judge who presides at the trial of the smugglers and sentences them to death."

"Oh dear," said Diva, seemingly alarmed and concerned at this news. "We're not actually going to hang anyone, are we?"

"Certainly not," said Georgie. "She'll just put on her black cap, like judges do, and say in a stern voice, 'You are found guilty of defrauding His Majesty's Customs and Excise, and I sentence you to be hanged by the neck until you are dead'. And then they will be led off the stage, and we don't see them again."

"So who is going to lead the smugglers, then? Major Benjy?" Diva laughed. It was not altogether a pleasant laugh, but Georgie decided to ignore the tone.

"Do you know, that was our first thought, but then we'd have to ask Elizabeth as well, and that would never work. I'm sure you can imagine the ructions."

"I suppose you're right. So who have you asked?"

"Well, I suppose I can tell you, but this is the bit I would really like you to keep quiet. We asked Irene."

"Irene?" said Diva in a state of some shock. "But she's a..."

"Not that anyone would really notice when she's dressed up, would they? Remember the time she did that hornpipe at the garden party at Mallards? The time when you were Mary Queen of Scots?"

"Oh yes, I see what you mean. I still think Major Benjy would be better."

"Well, as it happens, so do I, and do does Irene. But she thinks she has a plan to get him to appear without involving Elizabeth. But before you ask me what it is, I have to tell you that I don't know."

"And the leader of the Customs men?"

"The Padre, at the head of a troop of Boy Scouts."

"Hoots awa'," said Diva, in a fair imitation of the Padre's imitation of a Scottish accent. "And for me?"

This was the moment that Georgie had been dreading, but while he had been talking, he had made up his mind, and decided to bring it forward without reference to Lucia. "I thought you could be my wife – in the pageant, of course," he added hurriedly, in order to stave off any possible misunderstandings. "I'm writing most of the pageant, so I can give you as many lines to say or as big a part as you want. I'm sure that the innkeeper's wife was a great help to the smugglers when they were trying to escape the Customs men."

"Would she be hanged, too?" asked Diva. "I don't really like the idea of being hanged, even it if is all happening off-stage."

"I can write that you are sentenced to be transported to Australia, if you prefer."

Diva thought for a moment. "Yes, I think that's better than being hanged, when I come to think about it."

"Very well, then. I'll make sure that you have a good part that suits you."

"Well, that's most kind of you. And thank you so much for your idea about the horseradish and the lemon juice in the fish-paste."

Georgie glanced at his watch. "I'm so pleased that you will be joining our pageant," he told Diva, "but I really must be going. Lucia will be wondering what's happened to me."

TEN

Diva's observation from the bus the previous evening had not gone unnoticed. Elizabeth had seen the bus driving past, and was sure that it was Diva's face peering curiously out of the window.

"She won't have recognised us," said her husband. "Not dressed as we are."

It was true that the Mapp-Flints were clad in their oldest and shabbiest garments, which had never been beheld by mortal eye in Tilling, but Elizabeth remained unconvinced.

"Even though I have no great opinion of dear Diva's mental faculties," she said, "I have sometimes been forced to recognise that on occasion she possesses powers of observation that have surprised me."

"Well, what of it?" asked the Major. "Happily married couples such as ourselves are allowed to take a stroll of an evening, are they not?"

"I would remind you," said Elizabeth, "that you are pushing a wheelbarrow, in which are a spade, a rake and a hoe. Do they strike you as the usual accompaniment to an evening's stroll?"

"What of it? We might be going gardening."

This last was such a preposterous idea that Elizabeth did not deign to give it a verbal answer. A loud sniff verging on a snort expressed her opinion of this suggestion.

The pair trudged along the road in silence for about ten minutes more. At one point Benjy started to whistle a martial tune which presumably reminded him of his days in India, but Elizabeth clapped her hands to her ears and begged him to stop.

At length they reached the point on the road at which they must turn in order to reach the spot where the treasure was located. Benjy panted and strained as he manoeuvred the wheelbarrow through the dunes, and sank exhausted onto the sand when they eventually reached the dune where the chest remained half-buried as they had left it.

"'Pon my word," he exclaimed, panting, and mopping his forehead with a large red handkerchief whose colour nearly matched his face. "It's going to be tough work, Liz, getting the stuff back across the sand. It's bad enough pushing this thing when it's empty."

"Well, let's have a look, shall we, when you've finished your little rest." The prospect of the silk that she had seen earlier had energised Elizabeth Mapp-Flint and made her feel youthful to the extent that she felt, if not exactly girlish, at least of an age where a lady of reasonably advanced years might be considered to be girlish without appearing too ridiculous.

"Oh, very well," complained Benjy, heaving himself to his feet.

Together they removed the sand and driftwood that they had used earlier to conceal the chest, and lifted the lid.

"Just look," breathed Elizabeth. In the evening twilight, the silks glimmered and glistened, and their colours seemed more intense than they had in broad daylight.

"I'd just as soon have what's in the barrels we saw earlier," Benjy told her.

"Later, dear, later," Elizabeth cooed. The

dreams of dresses which would eclipse the most extravagant creations of Lucia, let alone Susan Wyse, Diva or poor little Evie, lent her voice an almost sickly-sweet quality.

The light was fading as she and Benjy took the silk out of the chest, and laid it gently in the wheelbarrow. There still seemed to be quite a quantity remaining; Elizabeth estimated that they had taken about two thirds of the total. Her mouth was almost watering as she imagined the entrances she would make to Lucia's and Susan Wyse's little gatherings, each time clad in a new and original epitome of luxurious splendour.

"That's enough, old girl," said the Major as the barrow was filled with the heavenly stuff, with a few bales of what smelled like tobacco added to the load. "As you say, we can come back for the brandy another day. There's enough whisky at home for tonight."

Elizabeth, who did not share her husband's ideas regarding whisky and soda, nonetheless held her peace. After all, she reasoned, if she were to start any criticism of his drinking habits, he was perfectly capable of simply refusing to carry any more of those delicious silks back to Grebe. Watching him strain with the barrow, whose wheel kept sinking into the soft sand of the dunes, she was well aware that without his aid she would be unable to maintain the effort, and there was far too much of the awkward slippery material to even consider carrying it in her arms. No, when they reached Grebe he deserved, if not all the whisky he could drink, at least all the whisky she would allow him to drink before starting to indicate her disapproval.

At length they reached the road, and the Major stopped, put down the barrow, and once again mopped his brow.

"Hard work that, Liz," he remarked. "I'll be glad when I can get home." He picked up the handles of the barrow and they resumed their trudge home, this time unobserved by any passing bus or vehicle.

Benjy carried the silk into the dining-room and laid it on the table there, before taking himself into his study, where he made a beeline for the second drawer of his desk, and poured himself a swift chota peg which he downed before pouring a second one and carrying it into the sitting-room where he ostentatiously diluted it with soda-water.

As his moustache was wet by the first reviving draught of that second drink, his feeling of peace and tranquillity was shattered by a loud wail of despair from the dining-room.

"The silk!"

The tone of voice was not one which could be safely ignored. Benjy hurriedly downed the remainder of his whisky, and made for the dining-room, where his wife was hysterically sobbing.

"Look, just look!" He followed her pointing finger and beheld yards of what had once been beautiful silk cloth, now brittle and fraying, stained with a hundred years of salt water, and creased with the folds of a century.

"There isn't enough decent stuff to make a pocket handkerchief," wailed Elizabeth.

"Maybe the rest of the silk in the chest will be better," he suggested.

Elizabeth turned on him. "There's no reason why it should be. And I was so looking forward to— Oh, never mind!" and she burst into tears.

There was nothing he felt that he could do, except pat her gently on the shoulder, mutter "There, there," and retreat to the study for a further whisky and soda.

ELEVEN

Georgie was a little concerned about Lucia's possible reaction to his independent decision to involve Diva in the pageant, but as it transpired, his fears were groundless. Lucia was not in the least displeased when he informed her of his invitation to Diva.

"What a good idea, Georgie," she told him. "It would be a shame for dear Diva to miss all the fun. And of course with her tea-shop, she will be a 'natural', as they say, for the part of the innkeeper's wife. What about Evie, though? We really must do something for her, especially as her husband is going to be leading the Excisemen."

Georgie noticed that Lucia did not seem

overly concerned about Elizabeth Mapp-Flint's part in the revels. "I think we should be able to find something for Evie."

"Some part that does not require too much in the way of speaking," Lucia said. "That little squeaky voice will never carry to the audience, especially out of doors. Perhaps she could be one of the Clerks of the Court in my— I mean the great scene at the end, when I condemn all the smugglers to be hanged."

"But that's probably going to be true for most of us. About the voices, I mean, not the hanging. Not you, of course," he added hurriedly. "I know that your voice will be perfectly audible to everyone. But I shall be so nervous about performing that I don't think anyone will be able to hear a single word I say."

"You have no need to worry, my dear. I am sure that you will speak beautifully, and everyone will be able to hear every word."

"I hope you are right," Georgie said, rather miserably. "I'm actually starting to find it difficult to get off to sleep at night, and we have three months before we are due to perform."

"You must adopt a mood of calm and tranquillity," Lucia told him firmly. "Do you remember what my Guru taught us in Riseholme? Breathing through one nostril and then the other. Such valuable wisdom he left behind. Om!" Lucia closed her eyes and her face assumed an expression that spoke of other-worldly spirituality.

"He may have left valuable wisdom behind him, but he certainly left with some valuable things of mine and Daisy Quantock's. And a considerable sum of Pepino's money, if you remember."

Lucia was unabashed. "Nonetheless, I think we all acquired some good from dear Daisy's Guru. Such an inspiration. I still have my Teacher's Robe in store. Maybe we should start Yoga classes in Tilling? Dear Diva and Susan would certainly benefit, and even Elizabeth might start to shake off that odious grasping envy that so darkens her soul."

Georgie noted that the possession of the Guru, who had proved to be a curry-cook from a restaurant in London, had passed swiftly and invisibly from Lucia to Daisy Quantock. In any case, it was ridiculous to imagine Elizabeth Mapp-Flint peacefully contorting her limbs into impossible postures and breathing silently.

"I do not think Tilling possesses the spiritual refinement of Riseholme. Yoga classes would be casting pearls before swine," he said to Lucia. He tactfully failed to mention that

Tilling also failed to possess the habit of following Lucia's lead in everything, as had been the custom in Riseholme, even when the subjects of their queen displayed signs of incipient rebellion. "In any event, we must concentrate on the pageant."

Lucia sighed. "How right you are, my dear, as always. Is there any more news?"

"Irene and I were looking at costumes in a book of hers. There's one for the innkeeper which would look rather good on me, I think."

"I'm sure that it will."

"And Irene was most mysterious about getting Major Benjy to play a part in the pageant."

"Doesn't she want to be leader of the smugglers?"

"I think she does, but she feels Major Benjy would be better in the part, and I'm not sure that I don't agree with her."

"But we can't possibly invite Major Benjy without Elizabeth," Lucia protested, "and it would be absolutely impossible to have her participation. She'd be wanting to take charge of everything and do it all her way. And we know where that would lead. Our dear sweet Tilling would be made to look ridiculous."

Georgie stroked his beard meditatively. "Yes, I see what you mean," he said. "Tarsome."

TWELVE

Elizabeth Mapp-Flint was distraught. It was impossible for her to decide which ached more; her hands and back from all the digging the day before, or her heart for the loss of what she had persuaded herself would be hers.

On closer examination, she had discovered that not all the silk was completely ruined. There were patches of the material which would make excellent handkerchiefs, or could be sewn together to create a charming patchwork effect. However, charming patchwork was a far cry from what she had expected to be able to create, and as for handkerchiefs – well, no one could be expected to make an impression of luxury with a few handkerchiefs, no matter how sumptuous or fine the material of which they were composed.

Not only had the silk proved to have fallen so far below her expectations that it might as well have fallen through the Earth and arrived in Australia, but as if to taunt her, the lesson in church that morning (for it was Sunday), which the Padre took as the text for his sermon was, "And why take ye thought for raiment? Consider the lilies of the field, how they grow; they toil not, neither do they spin: And yet I say unto you, That even Solomon in all his glory was not arrayed like one of these. Wherefore, if God so clothe the grass of the field, which today is, and tomorrow is cast into the oven, shall he not much more clothe you, O ye of little faith?"

This seemed to her to be most unfair. She had indeed had faith, in her Benjy-boy's judgement as regarded his belief in Puffin's discovery, and his skill and strength in recovering the silk, only to be dashed by an improvident Nature whose forces had dashed her hopes.

On the Mapp-Flints' return from church to Grebe, where an underdone saddle of mutton awaited them, Benjy sympathised with Elizabeth, but was unable to offer any practical solutions.

"I think it's time to try some of that tobacco," he said at length. "Should be nicely matured by now." So saying, he took himself off to his study.

A few minutes later, Elizabeth's painful reverie of dreams that would never be realised was interrupted by the sound of coughing emanating from her husband's study. At the same time, her nostrils were assailed by a smell that reminded her of a garden bonfire into which something unpleasant and long dead had made its way. She leaped to her feet as athletically as was possible for a woman of her age and constitution

"What on earth is going on, Benjy?" she cried as the coughing increased in intensity.

The door to his study opened, and her red-faced husband emerged through it. The smell grew worse before he slammed the door shut. He bent over, his hands on his knees, breathing deeply.

"My word, Liz," he said. "They must have been real men in those days to smoke that stuff. Took me right back to India and the smell of the funeral pyres in the morning."

"Enough of that sort of thing," Elizabeth said firmly. "I trust you have opened the windows in there."

"Opened as far as they will go," he confirmed, "and I threw the pipe out of the window. It should clear soon."

"So there's nothing to be done with the silk, and the tobacco seems to be completely un-usable. It was a mistake for you ever to have listened to Captain Puffin."

"There's still the brandy, Liz," said the Major. "I'll tell you what, while the smoke is clearing, I'll go back and fetch a barrel. Cheer us up a bit after all our disappointments so far. Coming with me, old girl?"

"I very much doubt if you'll find anything worthwhile there, and no, I am not coming with you."

THIRTEEN

Major Benjamin Mapp-Flint set off with the anticipation of the vintage brandy spurring him on. Indeed, it was hard to say which of the Mapp-Flints had experienced a greater sense of promise – whether it was Benjy's looking forward to his drink, or Elizabeth's desire to make an impact in the social circles of Tilling.

Once again, he struggled over the dunes and reached the place where the emptied chest still lay buried, one corner protruding through the sand. It was the work of only a few minutes before he had uncovered one small cask, which fitted easily under his arm as he made his way back towards Grebe.

Though he had sniffed hard at the little barrel before picking it up, he had been unable to detect any odour, other than a faint and expected smell of seaweed.

As he trudged homewards, he consoled himself with the thought of the taste of genuine Napoleon brandy.

He was so consumed by his daydreams, and the dreams of the money that would come to the Mapp-Flints when they sold off their store of priceless Napoleon brandy, that he completely failed to notice Irene Coles, sitting by the side of the road, her easel propped up in front of her.

"Hello, Benjy-Wenjy," she called out to him. "Good day for a walk."

"A fine day indeed," he replied genially. The geniality was largely the result of the anticipated brandy, but he saw no reason to make an enemy of Irene, whose acid tongue was considered in Tilling as a weapon to be greatly feared. "A fine day for painting?"

"The light's adequate, yes," she answered. "What's that under your arm?" she asked, seemingly noticing his burden for the first time.

"This? Oh, just something I found washed up on the beach," he stammered.

"I see. For a moment I thought you might be a smuggler, bringing in brandy and silks and tobacco and that sort of thing."

The Major was so shocked by this speech that he nearly dropped the cask. Recovering himself with a great effort, he let out a nervous laugh. "Oh no. Nothing of the sort, I assure you. Just a little bit of beach-combing on a Sunday afternoon."

"That's good. Of course, you could always use it to put your samphire in."

Benjy, aware of his wife's attempts to cover his initial excavations, could only manage a weak smile in reply, and raising his cap to Irene, continued on his way home.

By the time he had reached Grebe, and proudly deposited his prize on the kitchen table (the one on which his wife had set sail towards the Gallagher Banks in the unwelcome company of Lucia), he was more than ready to broach the cask.

Elizabeth had heard him enter the kitchen through the back door, and made her way to join him.

"Here you are, Liz. Get the glasses ready."

He turned the cask slowly, and let out a cry! "Here it is!"

"What, dear?" his wife asked.

"The bung. All I have to do is remove it, and..." He let his voice tail off in delicious anticipation.

But the stopper obstinately resisted his efforts to remove it. "Not surprised, really, after all these years," he said, as he attempted to insert a fork between the bung and the barrel. "Ah!" with a grunt of satisfaction. "That's loosened it."

A few more minutes' work, and the stopper was removed. He put his nose to the aperture and drew in a deep breath. "Can't smell very much. You have a sniff, Liz," he said, inviting his wife to try.

"I can smell something very strange," she said. "It's not a strong smell, but I am sure it's not brandy."

"Very odd." He found a spoon which would fit in the hole left by the stopper and plunged it into the cask. He brought it out, but rather than the amber aromatic liquid that he was expecting, it was covered with a dark sticky mass.

"That's not brandy," said Elizabeth. "But what on earth is it?"

Benjy gingerly took some on his finger and brought it to his mouth, ignoring Elizabeth's protesting cries.

"It's treacle," he said after a moment's thought. "Black treacle."

"Do you think that all the barrels are black treacle?" asked Elizabeth. "Do you mean that I've nearly broken my back, worn my hands to the bone – just look at my blisters – and trudged all the way to the dunes and back just for some rotten cloth, some tobacco that smells like I don't know what, and a few wooden barrels of black treacle? All because of some ridiculous idea of that Captain Puffin!"

"I can't say that I don't agree with you, Liz," said the Major. "It's dashed annoying. I was looking forward to seeing you in your new frocks."

This last was said with such seeming sincerity that the ice that had been congealing in Elizabeth's heart thawed a little. "And I was looking forward to seeing you enjoy your brandy," she told him.

"Well, it seems that we are both fated to disappointment," he said. "Foul stuff. This treacle, I mean. And the tobacco."

FOURTEEN

Georgie had just finished his breakfast when the doorbell rang. He wondered if it was the parcel of coloured silks that he'd ordered for his new cushion cover, and had just decided that there had not been enough time for the shop to receive his order, which he had only posted the previous evening, and send the goods to him, when Grosvenor entered the dining-room.

"Miss Irene's here to see you, sir. With a gentleman. Are you at home?"

"Oh, certainly, certainly," said Georgie, wiping all traces of toast crumbs from his beard with a napkin. "Show them into the drawing-room, if you would, please, Grosvenor. I shan't be a minute. And ask them if they would like some tea or coffee, please."

"Very good, sir."

It was a matter of only a few minutes before Georgie made his way to the drawing-room where Irene, clad in her usual garb of men's corduroy trousers and a fisherman's guernsey, was seated beside a young man dressed in what Georgie took to be the height of bohemian fashion. A vivid green soft-collared shirt with a bright red tie, tied in a loose knot, with a pair of light tan moleskin trousers comprised the bulk of the outfit. A rough tweed jacket lay beside him.

Both Irene and the stranger rose as Georgie entered.

"Behold my miracle," said Irene, indicating the young man.

"Yes... yes, of course," said Georgie.

"You are sweet," said Irene. "You don't understand a bit, and yet here you are as cool as one of Twistevant's cucumbers. Let me explain. This is Quentin Bontemps, one of the country's foremost theatre directors. Quentin, this is Mr Georgie Pillson, one of my dearest friends in this cultural desert that is Tilling."

"Pleased to meet you," said Georgie, taking the limp hand that was extended to him, as its owner half-rose from the sofa. He was none too pleased about the description of Tilling as a cultural desert, after all the work that Lucia had taken to introduce musical evenings, and culture of various kinds to replace the endless bridge evenings (though if Georgie were to be honest with himself, on balance he preferred the bridge; there were only so many times one could enjoy the slow movement of Beethoven's 'Moonlight Sonata'). However, being classed as one of Irene's greatest friends compensated for the other. She was, after all, one of the youngest ever winners of the Picture of the Year at the Royal Academy.

"And I you," came the reply in a voice that was surprisingly deep. "But Irene here has far too high an opinion of me. I'm only starting my career as a director."

"But you had excellent reviews in all the newspapers for your production of *Les Enfants Mal Formés*, didn't you? That's the play by the Absurdist Jean-Luc Garosse which was forced to close after two nights because it was so inflammatory."

Mr Bontemps looked a little embarrassed. "It wasn't exactly that," he admitted. "It was just that only the critics were in the first night's audience, and the second night—" He shrugged. "We didn't have an audience."

"But you still got good reviews," Irene insisted.

The response was a most unartistic-sounding snort from Mr Bontemps. "If you care to consider comments such as 'incomprehensible' and 'farrago of nonsense' as being good reviews, then yes, I suppose we did."

"Well, that's not the point," Irene said firmly. "The point, as I said to you, is that dear little Tilling is going to have a visit from a Most Important Person, and to entertain this MIP, there is to be a pageant. But what I didn't tell you is that this pageant is to be produced and directed by the wife of Georgie here, who has had experience in this sort of thing."

"Oh, you mean a pageant like that ghastly sort of Elizabethan thing that someone did up at that village called Eastholme? No, Riseholme, that was it. All the picture papers loved it. Complete rubbish, of course. Sentimental retelling of historical myths with no basis in fact at all." He stopped, suddenly aware of the expressions on the faces of Irene and Georgie. "Oh. Have I said something that I shouldn't?"

Georgie was still wondering how to phrase his protest when Irene spoke.

"You have put your foot well and truly in it, my dear Quentin," Irene told him coldly. "Not only was Georgie's wife the producer and chief architect of the whole thing, which as you rightly pointed out, was much admired by the press throughout the nation, but she also took the part of Queen Elizabeth." Mr Bontemps looked suitably abashed as Irene continued. "And in addition, Georgie here played the part of Sir Francis Drake."

By now, Mr Bontemps looked thoroughly uncomfortable, and shifted his weight from foot to foot as he spoke. "I really do seem to have put my foot in it, don't I?" There was no answer. "My sincere apologies. I confess that I never actually saw the production. I was basing my remarks on some comments made by a friend – actually now a former friend – who..." His voice tailed off. "In any event, I apologise most sincerely."

Georgie, who disliked any kind of difference of opinion, was quick to accept the proffered olive branch. "I accept your apology," he said simply.

"Do you have a script for your pageant?" asked Mr Bontemps.

"Not in any state that I am happy to show at present," Georgie answered, shaking his head. "We have some very preliminary ideas, though."

"A list of the characters?" suggested the director.

"That's easy," he answered, and with Irene's help proceeded to write a list, which he handed to Mr Bontemps.

"That seems very satisfactory," pronounced Mr Bontemps. "I can definitely manage that number."

Georgie began to feel a distinct sense of disquiet. "Irene, have you told Mr Bontemps about the present arrangements? I can see some problems if Mr Bontemps is to be in charge. I mean no disrespect to your abilities, but I foresee problems."

"Oh?"

Irene leaped to assist Georgie. "What Mr Pillson is trying to say is that his wife, who was the producer of that Elizabethan fête which you slandered just now, is expecting to produce this pageant here. My dear Quentin, I have not invited you here to take her place, but you are here to advise her, with all the tact and diplomacy at your command, with hints as to how things could be better managed."

"I see," said Mr Bontemps. "My dear sweet Irene, you may know me only as a bull in a china shop, but I would let you know that I can be a very sweet and refined bull, capable of navigating between positive mountains of Wedgwood without a single mishap."

"And there is another task for you," Irene continued, "which will also require you to become a diplomat. At the moment, I am cast as leader of the smugglers, but there is one man here in Tilling whom we all believe would be more suitable in the part."

"And what is the problem? From the sound of your voices, I take it that there is indeed a problem."

"The problem is his wife. She is an argumentative woman, who is jealous of Georgie's wife's position in our little Tilling— no, don't protest, Georgie, we all know this is perfectly true. If her husband is selected to play a part, then she will need to be given a prominent part as well. And that will cause problems. Is that not so, Georgie?"

Georgie felt that he had no choice but to agree, which he did, reluctantly.

"I see. In which case, my work is cut out for me," said Mr Bontemps. "But before I start, perhaps I might tempt you both to take a spin in my motor this afternoon, and you can point out all the sights of local interest to me."

"Too kind," said Georgie, "but my time this afternoon is already spoken for. Another day, maybe."

"I'll come with you," said Irene. "And I'll gladly point out all the objects of local interest, be they animal, vegetable or mineral."

FIFTEEN

Despite the heavy disappointments that he and Elizabeth had suffered following the nature of the smugglers' hoard, Major Mapp-Flint was convinced that there was more to be discovered.

The silks – well, there was little that could be done about that, sad though it had been for Liz to discover the condition of the material. The tobacco – well, perhaps it had been a mistake to expect tobacco to keep its savour after so long. But surely, he told himself, a smuggler would not have risked life and liberty simply to bring barrels of treacle illegally from France? There must be more than treacle in the remaining barrels.

Ignoring the complaints from his aching back, he started down the road to the dunes pushing the wheelbarrow before him. He followed the by now well-trodden and well-remembered path to the cache of booty, and started to excavate a little more. His efforts were soon rewarded by the sight of a dozen small kegs, slightly smaller than the one which had contained the treacle. He carefully lifted one out, and shook it, cocking his head in an attempt to hear what, if anything, it might contain.

He could just about make out the encouraging sound of liquid swirling within. He applied his nose to the bung in an attempt to smell what might be inside, though the barrel appeared to be sealed. To his delight, though he told himself that this was probably imagination, he could faintly discern a scent of something that might well be a delicious spirituous liquor.

With his heart bounding, he loaded these smaller barrels into the wheelbarrow. He covered the remainder of the hoard with sand, and made his painful journey across the dunes back to the road. Once he had reached the road, it became easier to push the barrow, but he still felt winded, and dropped the handles of the wheelbarrow, before seating himself on a stone wall and catching his breath.

As he sat, he became aware of a car approaching some way off, and, mindful of the earlier conversation with his wife, he became concerned that suspicion would fall on him if the kegs were observed. He leaped suddenly to his feet, his knee knocking painfully against the handles of the barrow. He only averted complete disaster by grabbing hold of the barrow to steady it and preventing it from tipping over. The noise of the car stopped, and he swiftly stripped off his jacket and used it to cover the contents of the wheelbarrow before turning his face away from the road to lessen the chance of his being recognised. The sound of the car engine starting up surprised him once again, and as it grew louder and the vehicle approached, he heard it slowing down, and stopping. A sudden blast from the car's horn made him jump, and he started, nearly dropping the handles of the wheelbarrow.

A familiar voice came to his ears.

"Benjy-Wenjy! What a delight to see you? Gathering samphire?"

Muttering under his breath, he turned to face Irene. Only one person in Tilling would address him so, together with the fact that she was repeating the stupid falsehood that Elizabeth had let slip.

"Yes, yes. Hot work," he added, indicating his jacket covering the contents of the barrow.

He could see Irene talking to the driver of the car, and he became aware of another face peering at him from the driving seat.

"Ah, Major Mapp-Flint," came a somewhat languid voice. "I have heard so much about you in my short time here in Tilling."

"This is Mr Quentin Bontemps," Irene explained. "He is staying with me for a few days."

"Indeed. Welcome to Tilling, Mr Bontemps," the Major replied, examining the other. From what he could make out at that distance, the fellow would give Miss Milliner Michael-Angelo a run for his money, what with his cravat and ridiculously coiffed hair.

"Perhaps we can give you a lift, Major?" the popinjay asked.

"Er, no. No thank you," he answered quickly. "Just my constitutional. The walk will do me good."

"At least let us take whatever is in your barrow. I'm sure it's very heavy."

"Thank you. Most kind. But no, I must take care of it myself. Never hear the last of it if I let it out of my sight. Know what I mean?" He winked horribly, and tapped the side of his nose in what he took to be a significant manner.

"Well, if you're sure," Irene told him. "Farewell, Benjy-Wenjy. Drive on," she commanded her companion in an imperious tone, and the motor took off, choking the Major in a cloud of dust and smoke.

A little rattled by this encounter, the Major took up his burden once more. Happily, he met no one else on his way back to Grebe, and he deposited the contents of the wheelbarrow in the gardener's shed. He was sure that he had taken ten of the little kegs from the hoard, but count them as often as he would, the total only came to nine. Casting his mind back, he had no recollection of leaving any of the barrels behind, or dropping one.

Scratching his head, he took one of the barrels into the kitchen, carefully opened the bung stopping it, and sniffed. The delicious aroma of brandy filled his nostrils as he carefully decanted a small portion into a glass. The amber liquid swirled in the glass most appealingly, and he took another sniff as the vapour arose to tickle his appetite.

After a final long appreciative sniff he took a sip of the most delicious brandy that he had ever tasted. This, he told himself, was worth any number of yards of silk. Liz should have as many frocks as she desired (well, nearly as many) with the proceeds from the sale of this heavenly liquid.

Even so, the thought of the missing barrel worried him. Perhaps, he considered as he took another sip, he had miscounted the number at first. Or, perish the thought, he had dropped one on the road and it was lying there still, waiting for someone else to discover it.

He finished the last of the brandy in his glass, reluctantly replaced the stopper in the barrel, and sighed as he set off once more to the dunes.

SIXTEEN

Quentin Bontemps's bright yellow road-
ster purred to a stop outside Taormina.
He hopped out of the driver's seat to open the
door for his passenger.

Irene emerged carrying her burden, and
quickly ducked into the house.

Once inside, she rang for Lucy, her maid.
"Lucy, go to Mallards and fetch Mr Georgie
here. Don't you dare let him tell you he's busy
washing his hair or anything like that, and
don't you dare come back without him."

It was only a matter of ten minutes before
Lucy returned, a rather flustered Georgie in
tow.

"What is it?" he asked. "I was just settling

down to my petit point, and when Lucy came in, I pricked my finger with the needle because she interrupted me. Tarsome. I hope this is important."

"It's not just important. It's very important. And it's very funny. Look."

She dragged Georgie by the hand into the kitchen where Quentin Bontemps was standing beside the kitchen table on which a small barrel was standing. A small glass was in his hand.

"Mr Pillson, behold!" he exclaimed with a smile.

"I am sorry, but I really can't see what I am meant to be looking at." Georgie sounded quite cross.

"Now, my dear, "said Irene. "Just sit yourself in that chair and take that glass that Quentin is offering you."

Georgie wordlessly complied with her request.

"Now put your nose in the glass and sniff," Irene commanded him.

"Delicious," was his verdict. "I won't pretend that I am an expert on these things, but that seems to me to be remarkably fine brandy."

"Why don't you taste it?" Quentin Bontemps suggested.

Following his sip of the brandy, Georgie allowed his face to relax into a broad smile. "Nectar, absolute nectar," he exclaimed. "Where did this come from?"

Irene wordlessly indicated the small barrel on the table.

"That is not helpful," Georgie complained. "I might have worked that out for myself. Where did you buy that barrel?"

"Ah," said Mr Bontemps. "The truth is that we didn't actually buy it."

"But we didn't steal it," said Irene. "If you'd come in Quentin's car on the drive with us, you wouldn't need to be asking these questions."

"You found it?" Georgie asked incredulously.

"Finders keepers, losers weepers," said Mr Bontemps.

"And who is the loser, then?" asked Georgie.

"Let us all have a glass of this wonderful liquid," said Irene ("Not too much for me," said Georgie. "I have some things to do later on which will need a clear head."). "Then we can tell you all about this afternoon."

"Well," said Irene, "Confusion to the French!" as she raised her glass. "Let me tell you all about it. We were speeding along, Quentin and I—"

"Not speeding," Mr Bontemps protested. "We

were travelling at a good rate, purring along happily, but not speeding. Definitely not." He took another sip of brandy, and Georgie wondered inwardly how many sips he had taken before his (Georgie's) arrival.

"We were purring along the road beside the dunes that goes past Grebe, when we saw an old tramp sitting on a wheelbarrow by the side of the road. Well, he must have heard us, because Quentin's car is a bit noisy—"

"It is not noisy! How dare you suggest that? It makes the precise sound it was meant to make when they made it," said Mr Bontemps, strengthening Georgie's suspicion that he had previously been sampling the brandy.

"Anyway," said Irene, "Quentin tooted his horn to warn this poor fellow, who obviously had no idea we were coming up behind him, and the man jumped a mile in the air, and something came out of his barrow. Then he took off his coat and put it over the barrow before setting off again. So as we passed the place where he had been surprised, Quentin stopped and I hopped out and picked up what he had dropped, and it turned out to be that barrel there.

"Then we started off again, and caught up

with this mystery man, and it turned out to be Benjy-Wenjy!"

"And very shifty he looked, too," said Mr Bontemps. "Definitely not keen on letting anyone else know what was in his barrow."

"How exciting!" said Georgie, leaning forward. "So you think he had a wheelbarrow full of brandy barrels?"

"Almost certainly."

"And where do you think he found them, then?"

"Well, I think we can be certain that he didn't buy them," said Mr Bontemps. "I'm not an expert on these things, but look here." He pointed to a wax seal on the top of the barrel. Georgie examined it.

"1810," he breathed. "Do you really believe this brandy comes from the time of Napoleon?"

"I believe that it does. And that makes it a very valuable drink. I have only once seen brandy this old offered for sale in a restaurant. You could buy a four-course meal for twenty people in an ordinary restaurant for the price the Ritz was asking for a glass of Napoleon brandy like this."

Irene whistled. "So this is worth how much?" indicating the barrel.

"More money than you or I could afford," said Mr Bontemps.

"And Major Benjy has even more barrels?" asked Georgie. "I'm sure that neither Elizabeth or Benjy has that sort of money. Why, they'd have to sell Grebe."

"So he found it," Irene said. "But where?"

There was a silence of a few seconds, broken by Georgie's "Smugglers!"

Irene's jaw dropped, and she looked at Georgie. "What did you just say? Oh, yes! You mean you think that Major Benjy is a smuggler?"

"Are you suggesting that Major Mapp-Flint is in league with a gang of smugglers bringing priceless Napoleon brandy into this country?" asked Mr Bontemps incredulously.

"No, no," Georgie answered. "He must have stumbled across buried treasure. Perhaps a pirate's treasure. Or perhaps a smuggler's hoard," he laughed.

"Perhaps not," said Irene, "but I am almost certain that this brandy didn't arrive in this country through the proper channels."

Mr Bontemps had been listening to this exchange, and came out with, "Didn't you say, Irene, that you wanted this Major to be the leader of the smugglers in the pageant?"

"Yes, both Georgie and I agreed that he has a villainous face which is just right for the part."

"So remind me once again, please. Why is he not already cast in the role?"

"Because—" Irene and Georgie spoke together and then stopped.

"You," said Irene.

"No, you," said Georgie.

"All right then. The problem with Major Benjy-Wenjy is not he himself. He's a decent old stick in his way – likes the odd chota peg and a bit too fond of telling us all about his days in India, but on the whole, there's no real malice in him. His wife, on the other hand—" Irene stopped and sucked in air through her teeth.

"A handful?" suggested Mr Bontemps.

"Both hands and a great big basket," Irene answered. "And she does not get on at all with Lucia – Georgie's wife. She would be in and out of the production all the time, wanting a part and if she didn't get one, our lives would be a misery as she nagged us about her husband's part and how he wasn't being treated fairly, and so on and so forth."

"Oh, the joys of working with amateurs," said Mr Bontemps. "Not that all professionals are angels, of course, but amateurs can be very

trying. Oh, yes." He sighed deeply before con-
tinuing. "I think, my dear Irene, and my dear
Mr Pillson—"

"Please call me Georgie." The fumes of the
brandy were mounting to his brain.

"And you must call me Quentin, please. But
don't you see? This brandy business gives
us the perfect way to get what we want. How
do you think Mrs Major is going to react if it
comes out that her household is a storehouse
filled with smuggled goods?"

"She won't be happy," said Irene.

"She's hoping to be made Mayor next year,"
said Georgie. "She's still incredibly jealous
that Lucia was Mayor the other year, and she
– Elizabeth, I mean – was only made Mayoress
to keep her quiet."

"And if it was known about Tilling that she and
Benjy were as good as smugglers, then she'd
never be considered for Mayor ever again. Oh,
joy! Quentin, my dear, another splash of this
wonderful stuff all round. And let us drink to
confusion to the Mapp-Flints."

She followed her own recommendation, and
Quentin followed suit. Georgie, while he ap-
preciated the brandy, felt it not quite proper
to follow the others' toast, and remained silent.

SEVENTEEN

Benjamin Mapp-Flint confessed himself to be baffled. There was a missing barrel, he was sure of it. But despite this loss, he felt there was still enough there for celebration.

"Liz!" he called.

"What is it now?" Elizabeth asked crossly, as she came into the room.

"Fool," he said.

Elizabeth grew red in the face. "What are you saying to me?"

"Your redcurrant fool," he answered, sheepishly. "Grandmamma Mapp's redcurrant fool."

"What of it?"

"It's delicious, but..."

"Yes?"

Benjy, sensing himself to be on the edge of a minefield, sidestepped carefully. "Do you remember one day when Susan Poppit, as she was then, served us with redcurrant fool?"

"I remember it well," his wife replied, with a note of acid in her voice. "It was the day that she returned from London with that ridiculous Order given to her for knitting a few bandages for the Cottage Hospital."

"Ah, but do you remember the fool?" he asked.

"I certainly remember the extravagance of it all, and you and that Puffin taking full advantage of the champagne and brandy – such wasteful and vulgar ingredients – in it."

"I was just wondering, Liz, if..."

"If we might use some of the brandy you have found to make redcurrant fool. An excellent idea—" Major Mapp-Flint relaxed "—if only we had some redcurrant bushes. In Mallards, of course, we could enjoy garden-produce of all kinds, all year round, but since Lucia's underhanded ways forced us to come here... In short, there are no redcurrants here at Grebe."

"Just an idea, Liz."

"And what are you going to do with those barrels of brandy? I trust you are not going to drink them all."

"Why, I shall sell them."

"And where will you sell them? To whom?" she enquired. "Do you really think that you can dispose of them here in Tilling without setting tongues wagging?"

Benjy, who in the past had been well aware of the power of wagging tongues, shook his head.

"You will have to explain where the brandy came from, and how you came across it. And who knows, someone, and I won't say who it might be, might have a word with the man she calls 'her' Inspector – 'her' Inspector indeed! – to ask some very awkward questions."

"So what do you suggest I do, Liz?" asked Benjy, by now somewhat rattled by the implications of all this.

"Put it back where you found it." Benjy's face fell. "Or simply store it in the gardener's shed."

"And the silk?"

His wife's face brightened a little. "I looked through a little more, and there are two or three pieces that might be used to make a frock or two."

"Then that's good news., isn't it?" A thought struck him. "But aren't you going to have to explain where the silk came from?"

"Of course. I found it at the bottom of a trunk of Aunt Caroline's which I had forgotten all about and I hadn't opened for many years."

Benjy considered this as a possibility, but there was no way that he could see that would enable him to spin a similar story about a dozen small barrels of brandy.

He sighed. "Very well, then. But I don't see how I can be expected to keep so many barrels of excellent brandy indefinitely."

EIGHTEEN

G eorgie had returned to Mallards, a little
intoxicated by the conversations that he
had held with Irene and Quentin, and also (if
he were honest with himself) by the brandy.

Quentin Bontemps had expounded his vision
of what the pageant might be, and Georgie,
loyal as he was to Lucia, could not but help
admiring the broad vision that was set before
him. Quentin had visions which approached,
if not actually exceeded, Lucia's dreams, but
unlike Lucia, had practical ways of achieving
his goals. So it seemed to Georgie after two
glasses of that delicious brandy.

Lucia, observant as always, fixed her eyes on
Georgie as they sat down to dinner, but held

her peace until the main course had been finished and the dessert of stewed plums was on the table in front of them.

"*Georgino mio*," she said. "Why so excited?"

Georgie hesitated. What he was about to say might well fail to win approval from Lucia. "I went to see Irene this morning," he began, cautiously.

"About the pageant, or about your painting?"

"About the pageant. And..." he paused to take a sip of water. "She had a friend with her."

"What sort of friend?"

"A friend from London. He seems to be quite famous."

"Oh? Another artist?"

"No, no." Georgie was becoming flustered. "He's apparently famous in the world of the theatre."

"Oh, how exciting! Did you tell him about my pageant? Do you think he'd want to be in it? What part do you think he could play?"

Georgie ignored the possessive that had given the pageant to Lucia, and steered around it as tactfully as he could. "Actually, he's not an actor at all. He is a director, and has apparently directed plays in London theatres."

"Oh." Lucia regarded her plums and custard

with an air of distaste. "And what did he have to say about the pageant?"

"I'll come to that later. Now I'll tell you a bit of news that will interest you."

"Perhaps," Lucia remarked coldly. "I had determined to put the shallow life of London behind me after that season that Pepino and I spent in Aunt Amy's house in Brompton Square."

"Ah, but this is not London, this is Tilling."

"Very well, then." She dug into her plums.

"After I had visited Irene, she and this man, Quentin Bontemps—"

"What a name!" Lucia interrupted rudely.

"Yes, that is his name. And if you're going to interrupt in that tarsome way, I shan't tell you the rest of the news."

"Ah, *poverino*," Lucia cooed. "Is oo vewy cross with Lucia?"

Georgie ignored this appeal, and continued. "After I'd visited Irene, she and Quentin went for a drive in his motor. And they were driving along the road between the sand-dunes and Grebe, and who do you think they saw walking along the road? Major Benjy," he answered his own question before Lucia could do so.

"Is that really so unusual?" Lucia asked. "He might have been going to play golf."

"With a spade and a wheelbarrow? And dressed like a tramp, Irene told me."

"Well?" Lucia leaned forward, clearly intrigued. "Was the wheelbarrow empty?"

"No, and that's the really interesting part. It was full of little barrels, about this big." Georgie indicated the size of the barrels with his hands. "He'd tried to cover them with his coat, but he must have jumped or something when the car came up behind him, and one of the barrels fell out without him noticing and they picked it up and put it in the car."

"Do go on," said Lucia, now apparently completely entranced by the narration.

"Well, Irene and Quentin caught up with him, and offered to take him and his barrels to Grebe, but he wasn't having any of it. So he went off and they went off, and Quentin opened the barrel."

"Don't tell me, Georgie! Oh, this is too delicious! Did the barrel contain French brandy, by any chance?"

"How tarsome," said Georgie, rather crossly. "I was just going to tell you that, but it was very clever of you to guess. Anyway, Irene invited me round to Taormina to try the brandy—"

"Aha!" said Lucia with an air of triumph. "I knew there was something there. But you're forgiven, my dear, since this is such an interesting story."

"—and it was delicious," Georgie continued, as if he hadn't been interrupted.

"But how would Major Benjy get hold of a lot of barrels of old brandy?" asked Lucia. "How many were there, did you say?"

"I didn't say, but Irene thought there were about a dozen, including the one that he lost."

"And where would he have got them from?"

"We – that is, Irene, Quentin, and I – thought that he'd probably discovered a smuggler's hoard somewhere in the sand-dunes."

"I see." Lucia removed a plum stone which had somehow entered her mouth and laid it carefully on the side of her plate. "Georgie, do you think that Major Benjy is doing something against the law?"

He frowned. "I really don't know. I think you would have to ask a solicitor to be sure about that, but if he's not going to pay the duty on that brandy, it's the same as receiving stolen goods, I think, and that's definitely a crime."

"Because..." Lucia had finished her plums and pushed the dish aside to make room for her elbows, which she planted firmly on the table, resting her chin in her hands. "If he is, then we can ask him to be the chief of the smuggler band."

"And Elizabeth?"

"Elizabeth will never know. If he says anything about this to Elizabeth, we simply let the whole of Tilling know about this brandy."

"That's not very nice, is it?"

"If I'm going to be honest, Elizabeth isn't very nice sometimes, and I know that she'd be perfectly horrible, not just to me and you, but to everyone, if she ever got involved with the pageant."

"I know, but even so..." Georgie thought for a moment. "Do you really think that Benjy can keep a secret from Elizabeth? She's terribly good at getting secrets out of people, you know."

"I think it's worth a try, though. Don't you?"

"I'll try."

Lucia seemed to be lost in thought for a moment.

"This Quintus Bonny—"

"Quentin Bontemps," Georgie corrected her.

"Well, whatever this man's name is. Do you think he might be persuaded to provide a little bit of assistance whenever I find myself a little stretched for time? After all, if I am to be writing, and producing, and acting in this thing, and then I have my Council work, and all the other work at the hospital and Sunday school and so on, I may find that there simply aren't enough hours in the day to do everything. And," here Lucia dropped her voice to a whisper, "I must confess that I am not as young as I was, and I sometimes find the pace of life to be a trifle too exciting at times."

Georgie, who had noticed an increasing tendency for Lucia to rest her eyes while sitting in her armchair of an evening, nodded.

"You do too much, my dear," he said. "You must spare yourself. And as far as Mr Bontemps – or Quentin, as I have been invited to call him – is concerned, I think that he would be very pleased to be asked to assist. And who knows? Maybe a fresh pair of eyes will be able to make suggestions to our plans which might improve the final production."

"As long as he does not turn the whole business into one of those modern plays where no-one speaks except in monosyllables, and the actors gaze soulfully into the audience most of the time." She shuddered. "I had quite enough of that sort of thing when we were in London."

"I am sure that he will be happy to assist."

"As long as he knows his place. You may invite him and Irene to visit tomorrow afternoon

— no, there is a meeting of the cricket club then, and I am President. Invite them for dinner tomorrow evening. Seven o'clock."

NINETEEN

The next day saw Major Mapp-Flint in the centre of Tilling. Elizabeth had told him that she was not "up to" the business of marketing that morning, and had given him a list of items without which, she gave the impression, the Mapp-Flint household would collapse in a state of total disorder and chaos.

To the Major's feeble protestations that surely Withers could be trusted with the marketing, she had answered simply that Withers was needed at Grebe to perform household tasks that could not be deferred any longer.

"Unless, of course," she had said, "you would prefer to clean the windows and scrub the bathroom floor, and send Withers into town to do the marketing."

Neither of these occupations was to his taste, and neither was doing the daily marketing, but marketing was preferable to the others, if only because it provided a chance of conversation.

After a brief and confusing conversation with Twistevant regarding the relative merits of various kinds of potato, whereby he was given to understand that 'new potatoes' did not refer to their never having been previously owned, and an embarrassing mishap with a mackerel at Hopkins' shop, he was happy to meet Georgie Pillson, who was seemingly on his own errands.

After the usual civilities had been exchanged, it became clear to the Major that the other wished to say something to him.

"Can we talk?" Georgie asked him.

The Major was under the impression that this was exactly what they had been doing, but he nodded.

"I have a sort of proposition that I would like to put to you," Georgie told him. However, it seemed that however much he desired to present the Major with this proposition, it was not going to be instantly forthcoming, as Georgie clearly found it difficult to express himself.

"Spit it out, old man," the Major offered encouragingly.

"Well, the thing is," Georgie said, a little less diffidently than before, "how would you like to be a smuggler?"

It was impossible for Benjy to hide his surprise, and it was only a matter of sheer chance that five pounds of new potatoes and a pair of mackerel did not end up on the pavement.

"Me... A smuggler?" he exclaimed at last.

"Yes. You know the sort of thing, barrels of brandy, and casks of tobacco and bales of silk."

If Benjy had been surprised before, it was nothing to the horror that washed over him now. Was he to be exposed to all as one who failed to pay the duty on these goods? Was he to be known ever after as Mapp-Flint the Smuggler? His best defence was attack, he decided.

"What on earth do you mean by that?" he asked, assuming a menacing air. "By Gad, sir, if I was not a peaceable man, I would call you out for that. Inviting a man to break the law in such a way. Positively insulting and preposterous!"

To his credit, Georgie, although he flinched under the onslaught of the Major's words, did not back down.

"Let me explain, Major," he said. "There will be a pageant performed here in Tilling later this year, on the theme of smugglers. As you know, there is a history of smuggling in this area."

The Major, who was all too aware of the evidence of these past misdeeds, nodded.

"And of course, we need people to play the parts in this pageant."

Benjy, who by now was beginning to see daylight, nodded again. "And you would like me to play the part of a smuggler? My dear chap, I do apologise." He laughed with a hearty guffaw which almost rattled the windows of Rice's shop. "I really did believe that you were inviting me to take part in a criminal enterprise."

Georgie laughed too, but his laugh was as a mountain streamlet, when compared to the full flood of the Major's mirth.

"Not just a smuggler," he said. "We would like you to take the part of the chief of the smugglers' band."

"Hmph. Well, I suppose I should be flattered by that." Benjy stroked his moustache. "Tell me more about this pageant. Tell you what, let's go into the Club. Had enough of this blood—blasted marketing game," he exclaimed, indicating the mackerel and the potatoes. "Care for a chota peg? Sun's over the yardarm somewhere in the world, don't you think?"

"Well... yes, I suppose so," Georgie replied. He inwardly considered that only the day before, he had partaken of some brandy in the middle of the afternoon, and now he was proposing to take alcoholic refreshment in the middle of the morning. Other than a small glass of wine at one of Lucia's Hitum lunches (for she had recently introduced the old Riseholme custom of Hitum, Titum and Scrub to Tilling society, and everyone, even Mr Wyse, but excepting Elizabeth, had fallen behind her in adopting these), he was unused to drinking in the daytime. He told himself sternly that this should not become a habit.

Once in the club, with the Major firmly ensconced in the large leather wingback chair by the window, with a large whisky and soda in front of him, and Georgie sitting opposite with a "Gin and It", both drinks having been paid for by Georgie, the conversation began.

"So, this pageant thing, then," began the Major, raising his glass. "Quai hai!"

"Your good health," replied Georgie.

"Now about this pageant thing," the Major repeated.

Georgie explained about the Royal visit, and the wish that the Royal personage should be entertained.

"And who's organising this, eh? Surely you're not doing all this yourself?"

Georgie hesitated. If at this stage he were to mention Lucia's involvement in this as the leading light, who knew what train of events this might set in motion? "Irene has a friend from London who is going to help with the production," he began.

"I see. It's all going to be professionally done, eh?"

"Well, he's not going to be doing all of the work."

Major Benjy gave Georgie a long hard look. "It's that wife of yours, isn't it, Pillson? She's the one running this show, I'll be bound."

Georgie could hardly deny it.

"What about Liz, then? My wife," Major Benjy asked. "She'll want a part in it. She'll want a part in running it as well, if I know her."

This was something that Georgie had been dreading. "Most of the parts for women have been taken," he started. "She could have a part as one of the chorus of sailors' wives."

The Major frowned at his empty glass. "Can't imagine she'd be very happy with that as a part," he muttered. He continued staring at his glass, but Georgie chose to ignore the unspoken hint. After a short silence, the Major bellowed "Quai hai!" at a waiter who came running, and ordered another whisky "to go on my bill".

Georgie plucked up his courage. "Does she have to know about the pageant at all?" he asked. "Could you keep it a secret from her?"

"By Jove, that's a thought," said the Major, sinking his moustache gratefully into the re-filled glass which had just appeared before him. "Mind you," he mused, "it's not something you can keep a secret for ever, is it? I mean to say, royalty, pageants and all that sort of thing. There'll probably be a newspaper johnny or two around, and she does like to see her name in the papers, does Liz. Why, that time when Irene Coles painted her and me and it was made Picture of the Year. Happy as a school-girl, she was. But if I keep all this a secret, and she finds out... I tell you something, old man. The life of yours truly won't be worth living. I'm sorry, but if I'm going to be the chief of your smuggler's band, I'm not going to be able to keep it a secret. There it is. Take it or leave it."

"I'm very afraid that I can't take it or leave it," Georgie said. "I'm going to have to talk to the others."

"You mean your wife, and that London popinjay you were talking about?"

Georgie admitted that these were precisely the people he meant.

"Oh, very well. But you must understand, old man, that as a married man yourself, we are very much at the mercy of our wives' moods."

To which sentiment, Georgie could only agree.

TWENTY

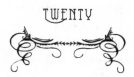

Irene Coles and Quentin Bontemps arrived at Mallards promptly at seven, having received the invitation to dinner from Georgie.

Quentin was wearing a velvet dinner-suit of bottle-green, which contrasted nicely with Georgie's ruby-red outfit.

"Well, look at you both," said Irene, admiringly. "The two of you together are wonderful subjects for a painting. Stand over there, Georgie, a little more into the light. And Quentin, a bit more to your left, closer to Georgie, if you would."

She pulled a sketchpad and pencil out of the capacious pocket of her blue fisherman's smock, and started to sketch the pair. "I shall call the painting 'Stop and Go', I think," she remarked as she sketched.

At that point, Lucia, who had been waiting in the garden-room, and had been wondering about the interval between the doorbell ringing and the non-arrival of her guests to greet their hostess (to say nothing of Georgie's absence), arrived in the hall.

"Lucia, dearest," said Irene, still sketching away. "Do forgive me. But just look at these wonderful specimens," pointing to Georgie and Quentin. "Don't you agree that they make the most wonderful subjects for a picture?"

"Of course you may sketch, dear one," Lucia told her. "But please don't take too long. Dinner will be served in a short while, and it would be so pleasant in this delicious weather to sit in the garden-room for a few minutes with our drinks before we take our places for the meal which we will take in there."

"Nearly finished," said Irene, making a few more quick dabs with her pencil at the paper. "There. I need a cocktail after that."

"And you shall have one, dear one," said Lucia, taking her by the arm and steering her towards the garden-room, Georgie and Quentin following in their wake.

Georgie mixed and handed round the drinks.

After they had finished their aperitifs, and were seated around the dining-table, Quentin Bontemps was the first to speak.

"Thank you, Mrs Pillson, for your kind invitation to your home. I must admit that I had never believed Irene when she wrote to me about the beauty of Tilling, and especially of your house, which she mentioned particularly in several of her letters to me."

Georgie stole a look at Irene, but her face was as guileless as that of a newborn baby.

"Why, thank you, Mr Bontemps."

"Please, do call me Quentin."

"And you must call me Lucia."

"Thank you. Delicious lobster, by the way. Simply delicious. Now, Georgie here has been telling me something about the pageant that you have been planning. But I would prefer to hear some more of the details from you, if you would be kind enough to tell me."

Lucia launched into an explanation of how the Royal personage was to be entertained, and Quentin listened attentively to her recital.

"Well," he said at the end. "It sounds extremely ambitious."

"Ah, but Art should be ambitious, should it not? Otherwise, can we truly term it Art?" Lucia looked around the table for confirmation, and was rewarded by the sight of several nodding heads.

"Of course. There are a few little things I might suggest, though. I really would advise against having all the Excisemen riding horses, for example. Believe me, horses are more trouble than they're worth."

"Are you sure?" Lucia asked dubiously.

"I'm positive. It's not just the performance, but the rehearsals you have to think about. Thirty horses each time. Stabling, feeding and clearing up after them. And some of your people won't be used to horses."

"It really would be much simpler for everyone if we left out the horses, Lucia," said Georgie.

After a brief period of thought, during which she closed her eyes as if concentrating, Lucia agreed. "How useful it is to have a fresh pair of eyes to examine our little plans," she said. "I am sure you are right. Perhaps the idea of having thirty Excisemen all mounted on horses was a little ambitious."

"I do like the idea of the women's chorus singing sea-shanties, but..."

"Do you not think it is a good idea?"

"I like it, but there are a few very minor points, where you might be able to enlighten me. Firstly, is there going to be any instrumental accompaniment to these shanties? Secondly, who is going to train and rehearse this choir? And lastly, though I have no objection in theory to a female choir singing sea-shanties, there may be some in the audience who have a different opinion."

"I see. I confess that we have not considered accompaniment and it may prove difficult to find a concertina or fiddle player. As to the second, I had planned to manage the choir myself."

"Absolutely not," said Quentin firmly.

"Why? I hope that you are not implying that I am incapable of doing that," said Lucia, stiffly.

"By no means. I confess to having no knowledge of your abilities in that area. But if you do that, as well as all the other work you are undertaking, your other activities will suffer. Indeed, if you are to rehearse the choir, I would strongly suggest that the judge's part be taken by someone else, if only to save you the strain of doing too much."

"I see," said Lucia reflectively. "How considerate of you to worry about me. Do you know," she said after a pause, "I do believe you are right. None of us is as young as we once were," she added, truthfully, if not altogether grammatically, "and it might prove a strain on the nerves. Perhaps we are indeed better off with-out the women's shanties."

"One other small point..."

"Yes?"

"I absolutely adore the idea of having the smugglers landing on the beach by the sand-dunes. So very atmospheric. And then having the judgement scene by the Town Hall. The perfect place, is it not?"

"So glad you approve," Lucia smiled.

"However, it seems to me that it might be taken as discourtesy to the Royal personage if he or she is expected to move the best part of a mile and a half between the different stages where the action is to take place. And always remember," he added, "Aristotle's rules of the three unities for drama."

"Ah yes," Lucia sighed. "Aristotle."

"And one of those, of course, was unity of place."

"Surely that referred to—" Georgie began, but stopped abruptly as Irene's toe made contact with his shin.

"Of course. Those wonderful plays. The com-edies, how full of Attic wit, and the tragedies of Sophocles and Euripides with their pity and terror," said Lucia, though it was obvious (to Georgie at least) that she had only the faintest idea of that to which Quentin Bontemps was referring.

"Exactly so. And though, as I say, I adore the smugglers landing their contraband on the beach by the dunes, I think that it will be much more convenient to the Royal personage and the audience, not to mention the smugglers themselves, if you were to stage all the scenes at the Town Hall. The words and the actions can conjure up the atmosphere of the seaside."

Georgie, who had previously disagreed with Lucia regarding the location of the various scenes, but had failed to win his case, broke in. "Quite Elizabethan, my dear. Remember that Shakespeare did not demand a sea and a beach for his Tempest."

Lucia's face lightened a little. "Very true, Georgie. Very well, we will move the action to the Town Hall. We can have placards declaring the scene of the action. Quite Elizabethan, as you say."

"I'm sure you will find both the performances and the rehearsals much easier to manage," Quentin Bontemps assured her.

"Not to mention the Royal personage," added Irene, who had remained silent up to this time. "Who knows, it might even be seen as lèse-majesté if you forced them to walk all that distance."

"Do you propose taking the part of the judge yourself?" Quentin Bontemps asked Lucia.

"Why, yes. Do you have any objection to that?"

"You do realise that at that time women were not allowed to be judges?"

"Artistic licence. I am a Justice of the Peace, and feel that I can give a fully authentic performance. And wearing a gown and a wig, who will know that it is I?"

"I am sure you are right, but you must allow me to direct that scene. I speak from experience when I say that it is almost impossible to direct a scene in which one has a part."

"Oh, very well."

It was clear to Georgie that Quentin Bontemps had experience of dealing with his theatrical peers and putting them in their places politely, but with a firm hand. "Iron hand in a velvet glove," Georgie thought to himself, and wondered if the phrase might somehow find its way into the script of the pageant.

Georgie then told the assembled company of his conversation with Major Benjy.

"Oh dear," said Lucia. "If Elizabeth wants to join in, then things may become rather difficult. She means well, but—"

"She doesn't mean well at all," Georgie said firmly. "You know very well that she simply likes to stir up trouble whenever she can. It's complete rubbish for you to say that she means well when she doesn't."

"If she tries to interfere, I can keep her in line," Irene pronounced.

"Believe me," Quentin Bontemps said. "I have not yet had the pleasure of meeting this lady, but I am confident that I can manage to keep her quiet. Working in the theatre, one learns a few useful tricks when it comes to lion-taming."

"For one thing," Irene pointed out, "we know that she and Major Benjy really are smugglers. Or very nearly so, anyway. I don't think she would like that to be spread about Tilling."

"I hope that none of us will be forced to stoop so low, Irene," Lucia pronounced gravely. "Mr Bontemps – Quentin – if we really must have Elizabeth Mapp-Flint as a part of this pageant, I rely on your skills as a lion-tamer – delicious metaphor – to ensure that there is no trouble."

For the rest of the meal, the conversation revolved around the business of being a Mayor of Tilling, on which Lucia expounded at length, and Quentin Bontemps listened with apparent rapt interest, skilfully stifling his yawns as

Lucia expounded on the theory and practice of planning regulations.

At length, the guests departed, and Lucia turned to Georgie. "Well, I think that Mr Bontemps will be the perfect person to put the finishing touches to our little pageant, don't you?"

TWENTY-ONE

The next day, Georgie was finishing his breakfast when Grosvenor came in.

"Excuse me, sir, but there's a Mr Bontemps at the door wanting to speak to you?"

"Please show him into the drawing-room and tell him I'll be with him in a minute."

"Very good, sir."

Tarsome, thought Georgie to himself. I wonder what he wants now. He finished his coffee, wiped his mouth on his napkin, and went into the drawing-room.

"I have a favour to ask of you. Well, actually, two favours," Quentin Bontemps began. "Firstly, is there any chance of obtaining the recipe for that divine lobster that we enjoyed last night?"

Georgie smiled and shook his head. "I am afraid that you will have no chance. Lucia's friends who have known her for years have been unable to drag that secret out of her." As he said this, he remembered the memorable occasion on which Lucia and Elizabeth Mapp-Flint had set sail together on a kitchen table, the recipe for lobster *à la Riseholme* secreted somewhere on Elizabeth's person – a recipe which she had stolen (there was no other word for it) from Lucia's kitchen while the latter was out of the house.

Subsequently she had attempted to serve this delicious dish, but the withering scorn with which it, and she, had been greeted had banished it for ever from the Mapp-Flint table.

"I am sorry to hear that," said Quentin Bontemps. "But everyone has their little secret, do they not, and it would be churlish to force them to be revealed simply to satisfy idle curiosity."

"Quite so," agreed Georgie, who had no intention of revealing the open secret of his toupet.

"Now my second request is connected with the pageant. I understand that this Major Mapp-Flint whom we surprised with his wheelbarrow full of brandy has agreed to be the chief of the smugglers."

"Yes, as I explained last night," Georgie answered, a little impatiently.

"But... the problem is his wife. Yes?"

"As you say," Georgie replied, not wishing to commit himself.

"Now I would like to meet this Major, and his wife. The problem is that I have no one to introduce me to them. Irene refuses point-blank to meet Mrs Mapp-Flint. And from what I gather, your wife would not be welcome either. Is that an accurate summary of the situation?"

"I would say so."

"So, you see, my dear Georgie, I am relying on you as my personal League of Nations to heal this rift in Tilling society. It is deliciously thrilling – I had no idea that such passions ran so deep in this corner of the world."

"They do indeed," said Georgie with a hint of a conspiratorial smile on his lips. "As I am sure you will discover."

"Very well, then. May I call for you in my motor at, shall we say half-past ten and then make our way to *la casa di Mapp-Flinti*?"

Georgie decided not to expose his Italian to one who, for all he knew, might be odiously fluent in the language. "Very well. I am sure that between us, we will be able to bring about a satisfactory outcome."

Half-past ten arrived, and Quentin's motor spluttered to a halt outside Mallards. Georgie, who had been waiting outside the front door, having previously informed Lucia of his plans, squeezed himself into the front seat beside Quentin.

As they passed the Trader's Arms, Georgie spotted Diva talking to the Padre and Evie. All the conversationalists looked up at the unfamiliar sound of Quentin's motor, and appeared to recognise the passenger with looks of surprise.

At the end of the journey along the marsh road to Grebe, which might best be described as exhilarating, and during which Georgie was forced to keep one hand on his head to prevent his new straw hat (and toupet) from flying into the road., the car drew up outside the Mapp-Flints'. Georgie hurriedly explained the history of Grebe (occupied originally by Lucia, but then exchanged for Mallards following some over-hasty financial investments by Elizabeth).

"I will try to avoid any related topics," Quentin assured Georgie as they waited for the door to be opened.

Withers, Elizabeth's parlourmaid, opened the door. "Oh, Mr Pillson, and..."

"Mr Bontemps. To see Major and Mrs Mapp-Flint."

"I'll just see, if you would be kind enough to wait here."

After a short wait, the two visitors were escorted to the drawing-room, where they were greeted by the Major.

"Ah, Pillson, and Bonhomme, was it?"

"Bontemps," Quentin corrected him.

"Ah, French, eh?"

"My ancestors were Huguenots, I believe."

"Liz – my lady wife, that is – will join us presently. She is out marketing, but should return within the hour. Can I interest you both in a drink while we wait? A small whisky and soda, perhaps?" he offered hopefully.

"A small brandy if you have any in the house, if you please," said Quentin. Georgie tried hard not to giggle at the expression that appeared on the Major's face.

"Brandy? Oh, ah, yes. Brandy," said the Major. "Perhaps... Somewhere... Are you sure you would not sooner have a whisky?"

"Well, of course, if brandy's too much trouble, a small whisky and soda would be most welcome."

"And the same for you, Pillson?"

"A splash of whisky only for me, and plenty of soda, please."

When the drinks had been poured and distributed, and appropriate noises of "Quai hai!", "Cheers" and "Your good health" had been made, the Major fixed Quentin with a stern eye.

"I believe, sir, that you were referring to something in particular when you talked about brandy just now."

"You are perfectly correct. When Miss Coles and I passed you on the road the other day, you had the misfortune to drop one of your barrels."

"Ah! So that's where it went!"

"And naturally, I attempted to discover what was inside it."

"And you succeeded, I take it?"

"I did. I confess to having sampled some of the contents with Miss Coles and Mr Pillson here, and it is certainly a very fine liquor indeed."

"Did you, by Jove? I hope you realise that I could take you to court for stealing my property?"

Quentin smiled a lazy smile. It was the smile of a cat which held a mouse between its paws, watching the animal scuttle back and forth with no hope of escape. "You could indeed. And then you would have to explain the source of the brandy, and why you were carrying so many little barrels from the dunes in a wheelbarrow."

"I might have bought it." The look on his face was one of near-panic.

This time, Quentin laughed outright. "My dear sir, I do not wish to cast aspersions on your financial situation, but we are talking here of Napoleon brandy – cognac which might even have graced the table of the little Corsican himself. Such a noble liquor does not come cheap."

A deep sigh from Major Mapp-Flint. "Well, the truth is that I found it buried in the sand-dunes."

"I thought as much."

"So, finders, keepers, what?"

"The same might be said of the barrel which fell off your wheelbarrow and into my possession." The Major's face fell. Quentin continued, "I hasten to add that my possession of the barrel is only temporary. I have brought it today in my motor, and will return it to you, together with suitable financial compensation for the amount of brandy that has been consumed."

"That's uncommonly generous of you, old

man," commented the Major, a look of relief replacing his previous expression.

"However," Bontemps went on, lifting a warning finger, "I should remind you that this brandy, together with any other items that you may have discovered, will not have been brought into this country legally. It will therefore be necessary for you to report it to the police, and they will no doubt arrange for the appropriate duty to be charged."

The Major's face fell once more. "And if I did not?"

"I suppose some law-abiding citizens might feel it to be their duty to inform the authorities."

"That sounds like a threat, sir."

"Not at all. Neither Mr Pillson, nor his wife, nor Miss Coles or myself would ever dream of such a thing," Quentin replied smoothly. "However, I cannot speak for the actions of others to whom the story might become known."

"I see." A silence of about a minute ensued, broken by the Major. "What is it that you require of me to ensure your silence? I must tell you that I strongly dislike being blackmailed."

"My dear Major Mapp-Flint," Quentin said smoothly. "I, too, dislike the term 'blackmail'. Shall we simply refer to this as a *quid pro quo*?"

"You can call it whatever you like. Just tell me what it is that you require of me."

"The pageant in which we are all taking part—"

"Hmph. I am not sure that I wish to take part after this conversation."

"Please hear me out. Now, I believe that our friend here," indicating Georgie, "has explained to you what part we feel you could play – with great distinction, I might add, having had the pleasure of your company. However, there is a problem in that Mrs Pillson – Lucia, that is – is nominally in charge of the pageant. In fact, it is more than a nominal charge – she has achieved miracles in going as far as she has. However, with the best will in the world, it must be remembered that she is an amateur in these matters. Hence my entry into Tilling, to ensure that the pageant shall be a complete success."

"Yes?" enquired the Major. Georgie, too, was puzzled as regards the direction towards which the conversation was tending.

"Now, Miss Coles has informed me of some of the history between your wife and Mrs Pillson. I want to make it clear," holding up a hand, "I am not attempting here to cast blame or aspersions on one side or the other. I do not care.

However, what I wish to emphasise is that if your wife has any complaints about the way the pageant is being directed, she is to come to me to complain about them. Mrs Pillson must be left entirely out of this. And if she wishes to gossip to others about the pageant, it is I who must be blamed. I do not live in Tilling, do you see, and I am perfectly content to be slandered and maligned by and to those whom I may never meet again."

"I see," said the Major doubtfully. "But where do I—"

"Your task is to ensure that your wife behaves in the way I have just described. If she does not, then maybe news of these little barrels will make its way into Tilling. Oh, and talking of these barrels. If you will excuse me?" He rose, and left the room before either the Major or Georgie could say a word.

"What an extraordinary person!" exclaimed the Major, draining his drink and pouring himself another.

"You must admit that it will make for a quiet life," Georgie ventured.

"By Jove, yes. Actually, now I come to look at the whole business, it's damned decent of him to take all that on himself."

Quentin Bontemps returned bearing the

brandy cask, which he deposited on the table beside the Major. "And here's a cheque for what I estimate to be the value of the brandy which we have drunk."

Major Benjy took up the piece of paper and scanned it. "My dear fellow, this is for ten pounds. How much did you drink?"

"Not very much, but I based the amount on the price one might pay at the Café Royal."

"Well, that's extraordinarily generous of you. Most generous. Another glass of whisky?"

The glasses were refilled, and as the three raised their drinks in salute, the sounds of Elizabeth Mapp-Flint returning home could be heard.

TWENTY-TWO

Elizabeth Mapp-Flint swept into the room, burdened with her marketing and what, from the expression on her face, would appear to be a foul mood.

"I would like to know," she said to her husband, ignoring Quentin Bontemps and Georgie, "who has parked that motor in front of our house. Such a ridiculous little thing. And that colour! I swear that if I were to ride a mile in that contraption I should be sick, if only on account of that hideous shade of yellow. Just the colour that dear Diva chose for her frock that evening at the Wyses' which made her look like a half-drowned chicken. Twistevant swore to me that he had no greengages left for sale, though I could see some behind him which he told me had been reserved by someone else. I had to go to Hopkins for the fish, despite my reservations as to his moral character. And the stationer had completely run out of the blue-black ink that I use for my letters. And who," she interrupted herself as she appeared to notice Quentin Bontemps for the first time, "is this with Mr Georgie, paying us, oh, such an unexpected visit? How gracious of you, Mr Georgie, to make your way all the way out here to the wilds of the marshes to pay a visit to your old friends."

Having delivered herself of this welcoming speech, Elizabeth heavily deposited her packages on one armchair and herself into another.

"I see that you gentlemen," putting an ironic stress on the last word, "are enjoying a quiet drink before luncheon. Might I be allowed to partake? A small dry sherry for me, if you please, Benjy-boy."

The Major leaped to his feet to provide his wife with the required refreshment, while Georgie remembered with amusement Elizabeth's words when she had been offered sherry at Lucia's first luncheon party after taking possession of Grebe. The words "No thank you. Poison to me," had become a popular expression of refusal at Tilling events at which the Mapp-Flints were not present. Clearly Elizabeth's susceptibility to the toxic effects of sherry was no longer a problem.

"Now then, Liz," said the Major as he handed the brimming glass to his wife, "Georgie Pillson here has brought his friend Mr Bonhomme—"

"Bontemps," corrected Quentin.

"Mr Bontemps, to talk about a pageant that will be held later this year. A Royal personage will be visiting, so I have been informed, and a historic pageant is to be arranged and performed for this person's amusement."

"Indeed? We are to have the citizens of Tilling dressing up and making spectacles of themselves, are we? I can just imagine whose idea this is, and who will take the principal part in this absurd scheme. Well, I can tell you now that neither I nor Major Mapp-Flint will have anything to do with this business."

"If I may," said Georgie, bravely entering the stream in full flood, "if you are referring to Lucia, she was asked by the Mayor to devise a pageant, given the success she had enjoyed some years ago at Risholme with the Elizabethan pageant. I am surprised that you, as a Councillor, were not informed of this."

Elizabeth, whose presence at meetings of the

town council was sporadic at best, sank back in her chair.

"Now it is true that Lucia and I have been working on plans for the pageant, but by great good fortune, Mr Bontemps here, who is a famous name in the world of London theatre," (here Quentin bowed slightly) "and who is visiting Tilling, has very kindly agreed to direct and produce the pageant."

"I see. More sherry, Benjy. And the subject of this *grand guignol*?"

"It will hardly be *grand guignol*, my dear Mrs Mapp-Flint," said Quentin, entering the conversation for the first time. "You must admit that such a genre would hardly be befitting to present to a Royal personage. No, what Mr and Mrs Pillson presented to me as an idea, an idea which has my full approval and agreement, is nothing less than a significant chapter in the life of this historic town of Tilling. That is to say, the days of the smugglers."

At the sound of this last word, Elizabeth gave a visible start, and a look of stunned surprise washed over her face.

So she, as well as Major Benjy, knows about the brandy and the smugglers. How very interesting this all is, Georgie thought to himself.

"I see," Elizabeth repeated stiffly, having

seemingly recovered from her surprise. "Is the story of lawbreakers and rogues a fit one to be presented to Royalty?"

"As long as the law triumphs over wrongdoing in the end," said Quentin. "I see no harm in the story. I think that we must all agree that smuggling is a crime that deserves punishment."

"Hear, hear," agreed Major Benjy, heartily.

"Yes, yes, of course," Elizabeth agreed. "Perhaps I was a little over-hasty in my condemnation. Would it be possible for Benjy and me to scriggle in at this late stage?"

"As it happens, your husband has just agreed to take the part of the leader of the band of smugglers. We felt that he was the perfect person to take the role." Quentin told her. "For so many reasons," he added.

"How thrilling!" Elizabeth exclaimed, clearly far from thrilled at the news. Indeed, her face betrayed traces of anxiety. "And for me? Might there be some way in which I might be able to add to this production?"

"I think," said Quentin thoughtfully, "that the existing script, such as it is, does not provide a suitable vehicle for you to display your talents. However, I feel we can write a part which is especially for you. You can take the part of the wife of the chief of the smugglers."

"What do you say to that, Liz?" exclaimed the Major heartily. "Excellent thinking there, if I may say so. By Jove, a part especially written for you."

"All I can say is that would never be the case if She was in charge. Thank you, Mr Bontemps."

"A pleasure to meet such a cultured and talented lady."

The conversation continued. An invitation to luncheon was offered by Benjy, and refused by Georgie on behalf of Quentin and himself, to the visible relief of Elizabeth.

On the way back to Tilling in the car, Georgie complimented Quentin on his lion-taming skills.

"Ah, but it's you and Lucia who will have the task of writing her part. Please don't make it too awkward for me when she complains about it. Mind you, there's a fine tragic scene for her at the end, when she begs the judge for her husband's life to be spared. I'm sure you can have fun with that."

TWENTY-THREE

Rehearsals started for the principals: the Padre as the head of the Excisemen; the Mapp-Flints as the chief smuggler and his wife; Irene as the second-in-command of the smugglers; Evie as the honest townswoman who informed the Excise about the smugglers; Georgie and Diva as the innkeeper and his wife; and Lucia as the judge in the final scene.

The Padre's band of Boy Scout Excisemen and Irene's collection of those of the town's youth who were not Boy Scouts were not needed in rehearsals at that time, according to Quentin Bontemps.

As the rehearsals progressed, Quentin Bontemps as producer and Georgie as principal creator of the script found themselves increasingly thrown together. The friendship between them, based on appreciation of the other's qualities, ripened, and it was not long before they were on Christian name terms with each other as if they had known each other all their lives.

Although Major Benjy made a fine figure of a smuggler, when it came to responding to his cues, there was often an embarrassing silence.

"She's blowing hard on the lee side, Captain," his cabin-boy (to be played by Twistevant's delivery boy in civilian life, but whose lines at these rehearsals were delivered by Quentin) would call to him.

The smuggler captain was, according to Georgie's script, supposed to answer, "Haul her in a luff, my bully-boys, and splice the mainbrace!".

"Are you sure that's right?" Quentin had asked Georgie when he had first read the script. "It doesn't seem quite the thing to me."

"I'm not perfectly sure, if I'm to be honest with you, but I have seen all these words in books I've been reading about those times."

"Well, it still doesn't seem quite right to me. Perhaps no one's going to notice," Quentin had said hopefully. "As long as there aren't too many sailors in the audience."

Instead of the instant nautical response that Major Benjy was supposed to provide, there would usually be a silence of about ten seconds, during which one might charitably suppose that Major Benjy was racking his brains. Following this, there might be an apology along the lines of, "I'm terribly sorry, old man, but I can't remember what it is that I'm meant to be saying here."

He would be patiently prompted by Quentin, apologise, and the scene would start again. This time the line might come out on time, but as something like, "Haul in a mainbrace, my bully-boys, and luff the splice," roared out at full volume, accompanied by dramatic gestures that would do as well for scaring off a herd of cattle as conducting a Beethoven symphony.

"No-one will notice," Quentin would say again, this time more with an air of resignation than of hope.

On the other hand, the original fears regarding Elizabeth had proved to be unfounded. Georgie had written her a comic part, and once she had grasped the idea that the audience were not laughing at her, Elizabeth Mapp-Flint, but at Mistress Sadler, wife of Captain

Ebenezer Sadler, master of the *Belle Rêve*, and leader of the Tilling smugglers, she took to it with gusto, even inventing bits of 'business' for herself.

For example, in one scene when Captain Sadler was unsure whether to go over to France or not, Elizabeth, whose script directed her to drive him across the Channel to fetch new French fashions for her, produced from somewhere within her skirts an undergarment which showed itself to be full of holes when shaken out and displayed to the audience.

Although the sight of this distressed lingerie brought blushes to Georgie's modest cheeks, Quentin Bontemps laughed and applauded Elizabeth.

"Well done, my dear Mrs Mapp-Flint. Excellent."

He was joined in his praises by Irene. "Good old Mapp! Wouldn't have thought you had it in you!" she called.

"Is this really suitable material to present to Royalty?" enquired Lucia, who had been watching the rehearsal, and following the example of Queen Victoria, remaining unamused. "Do you not find it a little coarse in nature?"

"Beauty and humour are in the eye of the beholder," replied Quentin. "Coarse it may be, but I will guarantee that the Royal personage will find something to laugh at. In the meantime, let us enjoy the spectacle."

Lucia was about to issue a sharp retort to this, but remembering that Quentin Bontemps was giving of himself most generously, for he had demanded no fee for the work he was doing, and showed no sign of demanding one, decided to hold her peace.

There was also the fact that he had praised her performance in her part as the judge only the day before, and had made some very flattering comments regarding her diction and phrasing. He had also made some suggestions regarding the use of her hands to express emotion and feeling, which she had, despite her initial resistance to the idea, found to be most helpful.

A scene with Georgie and Diva was the next on the list of scenes to be rehearsed. Despite Georgie's nervousness at appearing on stage, especially in front of royalty, Quentin's firm, but gentle, encouragement had helped him gain confidence in his abilities. He had enjoyed the luxury of writing his own part, and had avoided complex speeches and difficult words that would trip up his tongue. On the other hand, he had put in a few phrases in Italian, which would have seemed out of character for an eighteenth-century Sussex innkeeper, except that he explained to the audience at one point in his part that he had learned some Italian from a visiting sailor.

Diva had no problem with her lines, and delivered them in a clear strong voice ("Loud enough to be heard in Hastings," Quentin had remarked). On the other hand, she seemed to have trouble moving naturally on the stage. When she had to move from one side of the stage to the other, she would start off at her usual rapid pace, her legs moving beneath her like those of a Dutch doll. Halfway across, she would appear to remember that she was meant to be moving slowly and gracefully, and would suddenly slow to an almost complete stop, taking the best part of a minute to move no more than thirty feet.

"It's like watching a glacier in the Alps," Quentin said. "I half expect trees to start growing on her, and a whole forest flourishing by the time she exits the stage."

Eventually Georgie was forced to take her by the arm and guide her pace every time she had to move.

The Padre presented difficulties of another

kind. Accustomed to delivering sermons, his voice was clear, and carried well, but...

"Padre," said Quentin. "Is it really necessary for you to speak your lines in such a broad Scots accent? I fear that half the audience will fail to understand you."

"I dinna ken why ye're fashing yourself aboot it," replied the reverend gentleman. "'Twill be a guid thing for the royalty to hear the auld tongue spoken."

"It would indeed, could they understand a word of it," replied Quentin. "I really think it for the best if you adopt a turn of phrase that hails from south of the border."

"Oh, very well," muttered the Padre, and delivered his lines in tones which spoke more of England than they did of Scotland.

His wife, Evie, had the small but important role of informing the chief of the Excisemen (that is to say, her husband in real life) of the identities and whereabouts of the smugglers, thereby allowing him to catch them in the act of landing their illegal goods. Sadly, Evie's high-pitched squeaking failed to carry far, and despite Quentin's best efforts, she seemed unable to raise the volume of her voice.

"I really don't know what to do," said Quentin.

"She's been promised the part, and we need this part of the plot."

Inspiration struck Georgie. "I know," he exclaimed. "She can write it in a letter, which she hands to the Exciseman. All she has to say is 'I have a letter for you' and everyone will guess what she's saying, because it's so obvious, and then she can stand there and nod while the Padre – that is to say, the Exciseman – reads it all out loud so that everyone can hear."

"Genius, Georgie," Quentin said. "What a perfect solution. You have missed your vocation as a playwright."

Georgie felt rather proud of himself, and was even more pleased with his idea when it was put into practice, and worked perfectly.

But perhaps the biggest cross that Quentin had to bear was Lucia. It was not that she had set herself against Quentin and all his works; it was simply that her fertile mind kept sprouting forth new ideas. Having been dissuaded from staging the sea scenes on the sands, she kept thinking of ways in which these scenes could be made more realistic.

"I am sure those clever men in the bicycle shop could arrange some sort of a mechanism to go under the platform we're using as a ship's deck that would sway to and fro like a ship at sea," she said one day.

"I'm sure they could," said Georgie, "but I feel it would take them a long time to design and construct it, and then it would be rather large and heavy to move to and from the stage."

"But just think how realistic it would be for the actors," Lucia pointed out.

"It might be so realistic that they become seasick," Quentin pointed out. "And I don't think we require that degree of realism, do you?"

Lucia was forced to agree with that, and also with Georgie's advocacy of Shakespearean simplicity, but her mind kept producing ideas, as a volcano produces lava.

"I know that we said that we were not going to have thirty horses."

"Certainly not," said Georgie, firmly.

"But should not the Padre, as leader of the Excise men, be mounted on a horse?"

"We might manage one horse, I suppose," Quentin admitted.

But when the idea was put to the Padre, it proved to be impossible.

"I canna stand the beasties," he admitted. 'To be honest with ye, I'm feart of them."

"A donkey?" Lucia suggested hopefully, but that idea, too, was dismissed.

Naturally, the parts of the pageant that were of most interest to Lucia were the scenes at the end, where she, as the judge, presided over the trial of the smugglers, and in a long closing speech, condemned them all to death.

"How are we going to arrange the hangings?" she asked.

"The hangings?"

"Yes, at the end, the executions. All the smugglers are to be hanged, yes?"

"You are not suggesting that we hang them all on stage, are you?"

"Well, of course I am not suggesting that we actually do hang them. There must be some way that we could provide the illusion of their being hanged."

"I absolutely refuse to have any connection with the pageant if this is going to happen," said Georgie. "I think it's a simply horrid idea, and I want nothing at all to do with any of it."

"Lucia, I quite see how you wish the climax to be as dramatic as possible, and that you wish to show that wrongdoing should be punished by the law."

"I am so glad that you understand my point of view," smiled Lucia.

"However, let me tell you something of my experience in these matters. Very often I have found that action off-stage can provide a greater effect than if it is actually performed in front of the audience. The way that you put on the black cap just now and pronounced the sentence of death on the smugglers was magnificent. I felt a thrill of anticipatory horror running down my spine as you spoke those words, finishing with 'And may God have mercy on your soul'. Not only I was affected, I can tell you. Major Mapp-Flint looked completely stricken as he was led off, and poor Elizabeth appeared to be heartbroken."

Georgie felt that Quentin was exaggerating the effect of Lucia's acting on the other members of the cast, but for Lucia, this flood of fulsome praise was as music to her ears – music played by the finest orchestra.

"And so, my dear Lucia," he went on, "what I am saying is that you, through the force with which you have delivered the sentence of death on the miserable wretches before you, have inspired in the audience the pity and terror of which Aristotle speaks. There is no need for crude mechanical tricks. You have done all of that with your words. I speak as one who has made his life in theatre."

Faced with such praise, it was clearly an act

of superfluity for Lucia to insist on more realism, and she surrendered the point.

TWENTY-FOUR

Rehearsals went ahead for the "crowd scenes", as Quentin referred to them; that is to say, the Excisemen (Boy Scouts), the smugglers (the rag tag and bobtail of Tilling youth who had been recruited by Irene), and the townspeople (those of the shopkeepers and others who could be spared from their everyday labours).

To no-one's surprise, the Boy Scouts led by the Padre exhibited a sense of discipline that did them and their leader credit. When ordered to stand up straight and march, they did so, and by all accounts were an impressive force to be reckoned with.

Irene's ragamuffins, on the other hand,

showed a disappointing lack of commitment to the pageant. Irene's maid Lucy had to be dispatched to summon those who failed to turn up to rehearsals. Since Lucy was of the general size and build of a guardsman, very few of the absentees preferred to be absent for very long, especially after seeing two of their number forcibly brought to the rehearsal, one led painfully by the ear, and with the head of the other firmly gripped under one arm.

Once brought to the rehearsal, they showed a distressing tendency to find causes for quarrels among themselves, many seeing the assembly as a chance to settle old scores. The first rehearsal saw two black eyes and a bloody nose, and Quentin asked Major Benjy to enforce discipline.

"Now look here, you fellows," he bellowed at them in a tone of voice which had probably remained unused since the parade-grounds of India. "This sort of thing simply will not do. Stand up, you!" as he spied one of his gang lounging against a wall. Remember that you are soldiers— I mean, remember that you are brave lads, bringing from France those things that people need, such as... silks, and brandy and tobacco." Here Major Benjy noticed that one of his errand-boys was smoking a cigarette.

"But that's not an excuse for you to be smoking," he shouted. "Put that blasted cigarette out." He continued, occasionally forgetting to moderate his language, to the delight of his audience.

Faced with this barrage, the noisy rabble quietened. Chatter ceased, backs straightened, furtive cigarettes (for there were several that Major Benjy had failed to notice) were extinguished, and as far as an observer could tell, they were hanging on every word of their leader.

"Now remember," he said, "you are bringing freedom to the people of England. And like true Englishmen, you must fight for freedom."

These last words proved to be a terrible mistake. When the time came for the smugglers to be apprehended by the Excisemen, the gang, led by Major Benjy brandishing a riding crop (in lieu of a cutlass) and bellowing, "Up and at 'em, my lads!" laid into the unsuspecting Boy Scouts with a vigour one would not have believed was present in the usually lethargic errand-boys of Tilling.

The Scouts fled in whimpering terror, leaving the smugglers in possession of the field. The leaders of the two sides, the Padre and Major Benjy, faced up to each other.

"Your boys behaved disgracefully," the Padre accused the Major, forgetting in his anger to be either Scotch or medieval. "And there is one person to blame for it. You," he said, extending a forefinger, and prodding the Major in the chest.

"That's damn— dashed offensive of you to say that," replied the other. "By Jove, if you weren't a man of the cloth, I'd call you out for that."

"I will only repeat my opinion that it was your words, and your actions that brought about this," replied the Padre, indicating two sobbing Boy Scouts. "I want your boys to apologise to mine, and to make a promise that such a thing will not happen again."

At this point, Quentin, with Lucia in tow, intervened.

"Major, we must draw a line somewhere. I know that I told you that we wanted realism, but that does not extend to actual fisticuffs and the resulting injuries. If this had been a dress rehearsal, with your lads armed with their wooden cutlasses, I dread to think what the result might have been."

"Quite," said Lucia. "You should be ashamed of yourself, Major. The Padre's Boy Scouts are not your enemy, or the enemy of your boys."

"Well," said the smugglers' leader, obviously a

little crestfallen, and clearly more than a little astonished at what had just occurred. "'Pon my word, I mean to say, dash it all, yes I apologise. Maybe my words were a little hasty, but you know, once an old warhorse smells the battle and hears the trumpets and the shouting... Something in the Bible, isn't it, Padre?"

"You mean that passage in Job? But that's no excuse for encouraging your lads to attack my Boy Scouts like that."

"Shake hands," Quentin ordered them severely, and he was obeyed. "And now, Major, I want you to explain to your men— your boys, rather, that they are not to do anything like that ever again. The next time that we rehearse this fight between the Excise and the smugglers, the smugglers are to put up a token resistance only, and to lose gracefully. Is that clear?"

"It is clear," grumbled the Major, and went off to explain the new rules of engagement to his forces.

"And that, I think, concludes the rehearsals," said Quentin. "I think we've had quite enough excitement for one day."

"But you promised that I would be able to practice my judge's speech in front of the crowd," Lucia complained to Quentin.

"You may practice it to me later this afternoon,

with pleasure," Quentin told her. "But for now, I wish to return to the sanity of the twentieth century for an hour or two."

Lucia was forced to accept this decision, which she did with a good grace. Privately, she was thankful that it had been Quentin, and not she, who had been called in to lay down the law and keep the peace.

The next rehearsal passed without serious injury on either side, and the smugglers were led off for trial before the judge, who pronounced on their guilt in sonorous tones prior to sentencing them to death, unfortunately before the jury had delivered their verdict.

"Tarsome," Georgie said to Lucia later that evening. "I didn't realise you had to remember so many things when you were acting like this. He was busy putting the finishing touches to his costume as an innkeeper. "Is this too tight at the back, do you think?" he asked Lucia, trying on his coat, and turning to provide her with a view of the area in question.

"It appears to fit you beautifully, *caro mio*," she replied. "When you're finished with your coat, I want you to look at the sleeves of my robe."

Georgie dutifully examined the offending garment, and with a few deft stitches adjusted the sleeves so that they hung in a way that did not impede Lucia's hands.

"Now then, with the bands and the wig," he said. "Yes, I think that will do very nicely indeed."

TWENTY-FIVE

Quentin Bontemps maintained a professional air throughout, whether it was a case of patiently reminding Major Benjy of his cues for the tenth time in a morning, or politely considering and rejecting Lucia's ideas on how the pageant could be improved.

Georgie took the opportunity one day to speak to him about it.

"I really don't know how you have managed it," he told Quentin. "As we told you, Elizabeth can be extremely difficult at times. Sniping and carping at everything. And under your direction, she's as quiet as a lamb. What's your secret?"

"Stick and carrot, my dear Georgie. I never

let her forget, or if I do, then Benjy is sure to remind her, that they are sitting on a hoard of smuggled goods, and that it would be social death to them if this were to be revealed to the world."

"That's the stick. And the carrot?"

"That's the easy part. Within that unprepossessing exterior lurks a real talent for comic acting. Her sense of timing, and her sense of what will make others laugh are among the best I have ever encountered off the professional stage. Her husband, though..." He sighed.

"I know," said Georgie, miserably. "He looks the part, but if only he could remember his lines once in a while, and where he should be standing. I've rewritten his lines to make his part easier, but even then he seems to be having difficulty."

"He is improving slowly, though," said Quentin. "Especially when I hide his whisky-flask. Now your wife..."

"Lucia?"

"No, no. The tea-shop lady, Godiva. Your wife in the pageant. At least she can remember her lines and where to stand, but she moves like a wooden marionette. I do hope she learns to relax before the big day. And speaking of the big day, have we heard any more?"

"Lucia had something from the Mayor the other day. Apparently it will be the Duke and Duchess of York and their daughters who will be arriving by train at 9 o'clock. The pageant should start at half-past two, and should take no more than an hour or so."

"Half-past two. Good. They'll have eaten lunch and will be in a good mood, I hope. Is Lucia going to donate her lobster recipe to the council for the occasion?"

"What a good idea. I'll ask her."

"Anyway, they'll all be rather sleepy. With luck, some of them may drop off to sleep, and doze their way through the performance."

"Oh, I hope not!"

"Believe me, that's the best audience you can hope for. They will not cause any problems, won't notice if you forget your lines or trip over when you make your grand entrance. And they'll wake up at the end when the clapping starts and go home telling everyone what a wonderful time they had."

"So we don't need to bother?"

"Of course we need to bother. Look at Irene's painting – she's very highly thought of as an artist. She was the Picture of the Year at the Royal Academy, wasn't she? But do you think that half – no, make that a quarter – of the people who see her paintings know what they're looking at, or what she's trying to tell us with her paintings. They just think they're pretty shapes or pretty colours and that's it. But for the sake of the few – and sadly, it is only a few – who appreciate what she is doing, she must put her heart and soul into her creations."

"Goodness," said Georgie. "Do you tell her all that?"

"I don't need to. But the same applies to the theatre. Even when it is amateurs performing an amateur script – no offence meant, my dear Georgie, but you must admit that you are not a professional playwright – for an amateur audience. For the Mayor and Corporation of this dear quaint little Tilling, however worthy, are never going to reach the heights of artistic appreciation any more than the grand old Duke of York, and his charming wife and the two darling little princesses, not to mention the Bishop, whom I believe will also be in attendance. But there will be some in the audience who will appreciate what we are all trying to do – because I am inviting them here – and it is up to us all to make sure that they walk away happy and satisfied."

"Gracious me! That's an awful lot to take in.

Are you going to tell us all about this before the performance? Or is this one of your little secrets?"

"Don't worry. I'll make sure that everyone knows about it."

TWENTY-SIX

The first dress rehearsal (Quentin had insisted on two in order to accustom the players to their costumes, and to provide a chance for any errors of costume to be corrected) took place a few days after this conversation. By this time, all the players knew that it was to be the Duke of York and his family who were to be the audience, and all were excited at the thought of seeing the two little Princesses.

As the players assembled, their costumes were the subject of great curiosity. Although Irene had provided ideas for the type of costume that might be suitable for the pageant, she had left the creation of the costumes to the individual performers, and the result was a mixture of styles and of authenticity.

Lucia, for example, was dressed in her judge's robes, with some accoutrements borrowed from the Town Hall, and if the costume was not strictly speaking authentic for the period, the overall effect was definitely judicial.

Georgie's costume of a well-to-do innkeeper, on which he and Foljambe had spent time and trouble, basing it on the books that Irene had supplied, was a very handsome piece of work indeed. "In fact," Georgie had said, "I like it so much and it is so comfortable that I might start wearing it more often. Not for everyday marketing, of course, but I think it would be rather splendid to appear at one of Mr Wyse's dinners, for example, in knee-breeches and silk stockings."

The Padre appeared to have adapted some elements of clerical costume to provide an eighteenth-century outfit that gave an air of officialdom. Evie, however, had not been so successful with her attempt at a period costume, and her garments, in an unbecoming grey, made her appear more mouse-like than ever.

But it was the Mapp-Flints who formed the focus of attention. Major Benjy appeared in a great double-breasted pea jacket, with gold piping. His striped pantaloons were tucked into high top-boots, folded down at the top, and a broad leather belt encircled his waist, with a brace of antique pistols (discovered in a shop in Hastings, he explained) tucked into it, together with a large wooden cutlass. A large black beard partially covered his face, and the whole outfit was topped off by a tricorn hat, with gold lace edging.

Even Lucia, who had been prepared to cavil and criticise, was one of the first to congratulate the Major on the general effect of his costume.

"Truly magnificent," she told him. "I do declare that I am quite in awe of you."

Elizabeth Mapp-Flint was resplendent in a gown which, while not being quite of the period, nonetheless had an antique air about it. But it was not the cut of the dress that attracted the attention of the onlookers – it was the fact that it appeared to have been created out of the most beautiful silk taffeta.

"A very handsome dress indeed, Elizabeth," said Georgie. "Very handsome," he repeated as he took in the details. "And the colour is perfect. That bottle-green colour is such a match with those green feathers in your headdress."

The colour might have been better described

as matching the feelings of both Lucia and Diva, who had both silently priced the wondrous garment, and independently wondered from where the money had come which had purchased it. Not since the days of the ill-fated gowns of Elizabeth and Diva, based on a description of one worn by Mrs Titus Trout, had such a dress-related passion taken possession of Diva. And even Lucia, indifferent as she claimed to be about matters of dress, felt more than a passing pang of envy as Elizabeth swept past in a cloud of green silk.

"Better than I expected," remarked Quentin. "Always risky to allow amateurs to make their own costumes, in my experience, but I think you Tillingites have all outdone yourselves here. Well, most of you, anyway. Let us look at the Excisemen and the smugglers."

The Boy Scouts, as might be expected, were uniformly dressed in garments which, like the Padre's, suggested a uniform without actually being one. As for the smugglers... Irene had clearly inspired them, and a throng of striped jerseys and loose sailor's trousers was to be seen. Irene herself, together with Lucy, was dressed in a slightly more formal version of the smugglers' outfits.

"Excellent," said Quentin. "There will be no problem distinguishing who is on which side."

The rehearsal went ahead, and as dress rehearsals often do, it went badly. The novelty of the new clothes made Major Benjy forget his cues even more frequently than usual. The Padre kept tripping over his sword, which kept interposing itself between his legs, and the Boy Scouts kept giggling at his mishaps.

Even Georgie, whose costume was comfortable and well-fitting, found himself affected by the novelty, and he kept glancing down to admire the sight of his legs in their white stockings.

Evie was even more inaudible than usual, but Georgie's device of the letter meant that her message would be heard by the audience.

But the two heroines of the rehearsal were, in their different ways, Elizabeth and Lucia. Elizabeth swept around the stage in her silken cloud as if she had been wearing it all her life, and dominated almost every scene in which she appeared.

Lucia, for her part, was a perfect judge. Her carefully modulated Oxford vowels pronounced verdict and sentence to such effect that Major Benjy, standing in the dock (*sans* pistols and cutlass) was seen to be shaking in apparent fear.

"One more rehearsal tomorrow for luck," said Quentin, rising from the prompter's chair from which he had been directing. "It can only get better from now."

TWENTY-SEVEN

The second dress rehearsal which took place only two days before the planned visit, went as smoothly as Quentin could possibly have hoped. Played in front of the Mayor and Corporation (such of them who were not, like Lucia and Elizabeth, actually taking part in the event), the pageant drew applause and laughter at the appropriate points.

In addition to the civic dignitaries, some of Quentin's theatrical friends from London, whom he had invited to Tilling for the performance, also attended the rehearsal. Naturally, all had ideas for improving on Quentin's work, and equally naturally, Quentin rejected them all.

Elizabeth's "business" with the undergarment came in for special praise from all sides, however, and Lucia's judge's speech was pronounced to be "a little theatrical" by some, but in keeping with the spirit of the story.

Major Benjy was commended for his appearance, if not for the delivery of his lines, and the fight (now happily a mock fight) between the smugglers and the Excisemen was praised.

Georgie's script, for it was now almost totally his work, Lucia's interventions having been gradually excised as being too literary, and replaced by more comprehensible phrases, was commended by the London visitors, with the exception of the nautical terms. As Quentin had feared, there were some questions afterwards regarding the authenticity of these, but having spent so much time coaching Major Benjy to say the incorrect words correctly, as he said, "It would be a waste of time teaching him the correct words, only for him to say them incorrectly after all that. Assuming, that is, that I had nothing better to do with my time."

On the evening of the rehearsal, Quentin and Irene were sitting in the garden-room at Mallards, having enjoyed an excellent dinner with Georgie and Lucia.

"Shouldn't you be with your friends at the

Trader's Arms?" asked Lucia. "They will think that you are ignoring them."

"Oh, they'll be happy enough," said Quentin. "They'll be happier dissecting me when I'm not there. In any case, I am very glad to be here, because I want to say something important to you."

"About the pageant?" Lucia asked.

"No, but I am happy to talk about it later if you like. No, my news is about me. When Irene asked me to come to Tilling, I confess that I had no idea what I was walking into. To my great surprise and delight, I found that the town is full of charming and intelligent people, the hospitality of two of whom I am currently enjoying."

"I did tell you, Quentin dear, in my letter," said Irene.

"So you did, but I know how you sometimes exaggerate things."

"I never exaggerate," said Irene. "The plain unvarnished truth, that's me, isn't that so, Lucia darling?"

Lucia was spared the embarrassment of replying by Quentin, who quickly riposted with, "I've told you a million times not to exaggerate," at which Lucia, Georgie, and Irene all burst into laughter.

"But my point is," said Quentin, when the laughter had died away, "that having met all you wonderful people, I am going to find it very hard to return to London. In fact, to put the whole thing in a nutshell, I have plans to move myself to Tilling. I believe that there might even be the makings of a small renaissance here."

Lucia, who had promoted herself tirelessly as the queen of Culture in Tilling, was more than a little worried by this pronouncement. "We do already have our Art Society, and our little literary circle, as well as our musical evenings, and our dramatic productions, do we not?"

"Of course you do, and I this is one of the reasons why I am so anticipating living here. But what I am proposing is not to stop these things, but to help to lift them to greater heights. It is not a job that one person can do alone, especially as a newcomer. I will need you all to help me in this. Your musical evenings, for example, which I believe are held in this very room, with this fine instrument here. Now if I could prevail on my friends in London to write to you, Lucia, asking your permission to come and give a small recital, in this room, on this instrument? And without boasting, I can say that some of my friends are highly accomplished professional musicians."

Lucia's imagination soared. She could imagine these shining stars of the musical world visiting Mallards, partaking of a light but nourishing supper, complete with entertaining musical anecdotes, and then proceeding to the garden-room where they would enchant the evening, and the select few who would be invited, with their renditions of the finest classical music. And then... perhaps at the end of their playing, there would be a murmur from the audience, and Lucia would murmur back in a self-deprecating tone, "If you insist," and drift over to the piano, from which would then issue those triplets that heralded the first movement of noble Beethoven's Sonata in C# minor, often called the "Moonlight".

She nodded, and Quentin continued. "Now as regards the dramatic arts, I can say now that I never expected to find such a wealth of talent here in Tilling. And all the hard work that you had done before I arrived made my life so much easier. I really would love to work with you again in the same way on other future productions."

Having seen how Quentin had brought her vision of the pageant to such successful life, and with the flattery that was being bestowed on her, Lucia had little to argue with. Perhaps, she mused, Quentin might be persuaded to work his magic on a production of *Macbeth*, in which she could play Lady Macbeth and speak her famous sleepwalking soliloquy, with the veiled soul-horror giving life to her words.

"As for art, Irene tells me that you and Georgie are among the leading artistic lights of the town. But with all due respect, you are not professional artists in the same class as Irene. But what if, and I put this forward with all due hesitancy, at your Art Society exhibitions, Irene invites one of her Royal Academy friends to give a masterclass?"

"I do like that idea," said Georgie warmly. "I know that you have given me some help in the past, Irene, but I do think that my painting needs a fresh approach."

"Good for you, Georgie," Irene applauded him. "Keep trying new things. Who knows what the result might be?"

"I'm putting this all very badly," Quentin said. "What I am trying to say is that I don't want to upset the apple-cart. I just want to be around, giving a hand here, a little push there, and generally helping to put Tilling on the map. This pageant is going to be the start. I've invited the drama critics from all the London dailies to come along, to begin with."

"Oh dear," said Georgie. "I wish you hadn't told me that. Now I shall be dreadfully nervous, even more than with the Duke and Duchess and the two little Princesses."

"Ignore them," said Quentin. "It's what I always did when I was on the stage in London. You see them with their notebooks and pencils, sitting in the stalls, and you think to yourself, 'I'm here on stage and you're not. People are paying to see me, not you. If I wasn't here, you wouldn't be here either.'"

"And that works?"

"Every time," Quentin assured him. "I've never tried it with royalty, but I'm sure it works just as well with them as it does with critics."

Lucia had been considering all this, and had come to the conclusion that if there were to be battles to seize the artistic high ground, it was more than likely that she would emerge as the loser. Much better, she felt, to work with Quentin, at least at the start. She grudgingly admitted to herself that he had, after all, brought something to the pageant that she could never have done, and without ruffling too many feathers, including hers. Her tactics would be based on welcome and cooperation rather than competition.

"Where will you live?" she asked Quentin.

"As you know, I'm staying with Irene at the moment, but that can hardly be permanent. I am sure that I will be able to find some perfectly delicious little place I can call my own, though."

"The man who bought Captain Puffin's house after he died – I mean that Captain Puffin died, not the man who bought the house," Irene began. Lucia felt that Irene had perhaps enjoyed one or two cocktails too many. "Anyway, he moved out – not Captain Puffin, but the other one I'm talking about. Last week. Or perhaps the week before." She put her elbows on the table and sighed. "What I'm saying is that Captain Puffin's house is empty. But it's not been Captain Puffin's house since he died, of course."

"And I'm sure it's freehold," said Georgie

"Which house is that, then?" Quentin asked.

"I'll show you," Georgie said, bringing him to the garden-room window and pointing out the house.

"So close. Wonderful!" said Quentin, in a sort of ecstasy. "As soon as this pageant is over, I will make my way to the agents and see about buying the place."

"How exciting!" said Georgie. "I do believe that you will be a full Tillingite before you know it."

Irene had obviously been thinking about something else. "Where did she find it?" she asked.

"Where did who find what?" asked Georgie.

"Where did Mapp find that silk?" Irene asked. "The silk she used to make her dress. The green one."

"I don't know much about these things," said Quentin, "but it didn't look new to me, somehow."

Irene stood up suddenly and spread her arms wide. "Silly silly me!" she said. "She smuggled it. Along with the brandy."

"Do you know, I think you're right," said Georgie. "That colour of green isn't in fashion nowadays." Georgie spoke with conviction, being quite knowledgeable about female dress. "Well, fancy that."

Quentin had gone into fits of helpless giggles. "Oh, this is all too priceless," he wheezed. "Here's a pageant about smugglers, and the principals in the plot think themselves to be no better than smugglers."

"What do you mean?" Lucia asked sharply. "They are smugglers, aren't they?"

Quentin had by now got his laughter under control. "I'll explain after the performance," he said.

"Well, I think it's very tarsome of you not to let us in on the joke," said Georgie.

"It will spoil everything if I tell you now. Please, forgive me, and have patience."

"Oh, very well," said Georgie.

TWENTY-EIGHT

The day of the performance dawned. The
weather was bright and promised fair, according to those who claimed to understand
such things. The visitors were due to arrive by
special train at ten o'clock, and the principals
of the pageant held an early morning discus-
sion as to whether the Royal party should be
greeted at the station by the cast in costume.

"I really don't think I could manage it," said
Diva. "I'm nervous enough going on stage
dressed like that, and I don't think I could
possibly make my way through the streets of
Tilling."

"I agree," Georgie told them. "It's a lovely costume that I am wearing, but I'm not really sure

now if it is for everyday wear, even for dukes and duchesses and princesses."

Major Benjy and Elizabeth had come up to town from Grebe early, bearing their costumes. Lucia had generously allowed them the use of the spare room at Mallards to change prior to the performance. Elizabeth had been less than enthusiastic, sniffing that it was no hardship for Lucia to make this offer, but Major Benjy had been all in favour.

"Think of that silk, Liz," he had said to her. "You don't want to be getting mud and dust all over it walking from Grebe into the town." So she had capitulated with a bad grace, and the wondrous silk garment, together with the undergarment which was to be produced later, and Major Benjy's costume, including his cutlass and pistols, had all been transported to Mallards the previous evening.

"I vote for meeting them in costume," said the Major.

"I dinna think that's a bonny idea," said the Padre.

"Eh? Why?"

"Aye, with your pistols and sword and a' that, they might reckon ye're up to nae guid. They might take ye awa.'"

"I see what you mean," the Major answered,

after giving the matter some thought. "Perhaps better not to go in costume."

"Certainly not," said Quentin, who had joined the group, unnoticed until that moment. "The costumes must be a surprise for the audience, like the words and your acting. Now, I am unable to offer you any hospitality myself, since I do not possess my own residence in Tilling – as yet, anyway – and the inns are full of tourists and newspaper reporters and theatre critics and the like, but Mr and Mrs Pillson have very kindly offered to provide us with an early luncheon at Mallards House, should you wish to partake. But before that, I very much wish to say a few words to you, so if we can all assemble in the garden of Mallards House in a few minutes, that will be a convenient place, far from the madding crowd that we hope will be our audience today."

As he moved off, Elizabeth was heard to mutter, "Mallards House indeed! Simple Mallards was good enough when I lived there." But this was an old complaint, and no one appeared inclined to notice.

The group moved to Mallards, and into the garden, where they awaited the arrival of Quentin Bontemps. As he had promised Georgie earlier, he exhorted them to do their best, and to make sure that the portion of the audience which would appreciate their performance really had something to admire.

"Who is nervous?" he asked.

All expressed their fear of performing. "Don't worry," Quentin told them. "Today is your day, not theirs. If you enjoy yourselves, the audience will enjoy it. If you are scared and miserable, the audience will be miserable. The rehearsal the other was good – very good indeed. Don't believe that nonsense about a good rehearsal meaning a bad performance. Today is going to be better than the rehearsal. Now, I suggest you all have something to eat. Not too much, and certainly not too much to drink. But you can't act well on an empty stomach. I speak from experience. Eat first, change into your costumes, and them out there and break a leg."

"Why would he want us to break our legs?' Diva asked Georgie as they drifted towards the garden-room, where Grosvenor and Foljambe had prepared an appetising buffet.

"It's tradition in the theatre," Georgie told her. "If you wish someone good luck, then the imps of the theatre will thwart your wish. So you wish them bad luck, to confuse the imps, who will then bring you good luck, to thwart your wish for bad luck."

"I see, I think," Diva said doubtfully. "It does seem rather a strange idea, though."

Though all professed to be nervous and to have very little appetite, the sandwiches and other *hors d'œuvres* quickly disappeared.

Elizabeth, who had been in hopes of discovering something inedible and leaving it ostentatiously uneaten, found herself disappointed, and had eaten four fish-paste and cucumber sandwiches and three chicken *vol au vents* before remembering that she had to fit into her new silk dress in a matter of an hour or so.

Eventually, all retired to change and re-assemble in the Town Hall, which was to act as the "wings" of the stage, where they awaited their cues together with the Excisemen, the smugglers, and the townsfolk.

At half-past two, the Town Clerk poked his head around the door of the council chamber where they were waiting, to announce that the Royal party had taken their places.

"You're on," Quentin told Major Benjy and Elizabeth, who were to open the pageant, with a scene where she sends him off to sea to fetch her some new clothes. The others could only hear the sound of applause as the couple came on stage, followed by the sound of the actors' voices. Suddenly there was a roar of laughter and applause from the audience.

"Elizabeth's just shown her bloomers to the world," remarked Irene.

"Get ready, innkeeper and wife," Quentin reminded Georgie and Diva.

Much to his surprise, Georgie was not nervous. Quentin had rehearsed the cast so well that Georgie's movements felt natural, and for once, Diva moved naturally as the script directed. As the innkeeper (Georgie) spoke to the leader of the smugglers (Major Benjy), he noticed that the latter was swaying slightly, and there was a slightly glazed look in his eye.

"I do hope that he hasn't been sampling his brandy," Georgie thought to himself, though he had a horrible feeling that this might be the case.

The scene ended, and the Padre at the head of his Boy Scouts took the stage before Evie entered, and informed the forces of law and order of the whereabouts of the smugglers.

Next came the scene at sea, for which Lucia had wanted a rolling deck, failing the attempt to stage it on the seashore. Major Benjy bellowed out his best nautical lines, his smugglers, under Irene's direction, shivered their timbers, took in their luffs, and spliced their mainbraces to perfection before landing their cargo of contraband from their boat.

The Excisemen entered, and the battle scene followed. A slight mishap occurred when the wooden blade of Major Benjy's cutlass, which he had been waving energetically to encourage his smugglers, parted company from the hilt, and went flying into the audience, happily in a different direction from the Royal party. Undeterred, the Major let out what appeared to be a Hindustani oath (at any event, no one could understand or repeat what he said) and charged forward, a pistol in one hand, and the hilt of the sword grasped firmly in the other. The fight was soon over, happily with no injuries incurred on either side, and the scene changed to the courtroom.

Lucia was the centre of attention as, bewigged and robed, she took her place, and the court proceedings opened.

The jury quickly found the smugglers guilty, and it was time for Lucia's great speech, which Georgie had written for her. As she put the black cap on her head, there was silence, which lasted until her final "And may God have mercy on your souls" following which Elizabeth burst into a fit of very realistic tearful appeals for mercy, and to everyone's amazement, some sobs were heard from the audience.

This was the final scene, and all the performers came onto the stage to make their bows to rapturous applause from the audience. Georgie looked around the audience, and to his surprise found himself looking into the eyes of the Duchess of York. Taken aback, he bowed slightly in her direction, a greeting which was returned with a flutter of the ducal gloved hand.

Following this curtain call, the performers retired to the council chamber, and were preparing to leave to change from their costumes when Quentin stopped them.

"Not yet," he said. "We are expecting visitors."

And at that moment, the Duke and Duchess, along with the two little Princesses, the Bishop, and what seemed like a host of equerries entered.

Lucia remembered how to curtsey from her days in London and performed a most creditable obeisance. Elizabeth's effort was sadly handicapped by the silk in which she was cocooned, and Diva's and Evie's curtseys were presumably taken in the spirit with which they were performed, rather than being judged on their actual execution.

Georgie, the Padre, and Major Benjy all removed their hats and made low bows, as the Royal personages moved towards them, and exchanged a few words with each of the performers.

Georgie was terribly embarrassed when the Duke asked him if he and Diva were married in real life, but managed to stammer out that he was, in fact, married to the judge who had passed sentence on the smugglers.

Major Benjy turned bright pink with embarrassment when the Duchess complimented him on the way he had led the smugglers and expressed her hope that the cutlass that had parted company with its hilt had not injured any members of the audience.

The Padre seemed taken aback when the Bishop humorously asked him if he intended to change profession.

Lucia was told by the elder of the little princesses that she was "very frightening", which she took as a compliment to her Thespian skills.

Much to Irene's surprise, the Duchess instantly saw through her male disguise and recognised her as the artist who had painted the Picture of the Year at the Royal Academy, where they had met previously.

Quentin Bontemps was likewise compliment-ed heartily, but protested that the glory really belonged to the residents of Tilling, and then the Royal personages departed.

"Well done, everybody," Quentin praised them. "If you will excuse me, I must go and find the critics, and make sure that they spell everyone's names correctly in tomorrow's newspapers."

TWENTY-NINE

The next day's newspapers were all that Tilling could have hoped for. As might be expected, the Duke and Duchess of York formed the main theme of the story, but the pageant was featured prominently.

Several of the papers had printed photographs, and Major Benjy formed the centrepiece of one, striking a fearsome pose. As Quentin had promised, all the names were spelled correctly and the reports were glowing.

"If only some of my London productions had had these notices," he said to Georgie when he appeared with an armful of newspapers. "Just look here. 'One could almost believe these were professional actors.' And here. 'There was comedy, action, and at the end, elements of pure pathos as the black cap was donned, and the malefactors taken to meet their doom.' This one. 'Credit must be given to Major Benjamin Mapp-Flint, who filled the air with scraps of nautical language as he rallied his men against the Excisemen.' And this is for you, my dear Georgie. Read it."

Georgie took the newspaper and read out, "'The script of the pageant was largely the work of Mr George Pillson (the husband of Emmeline "Lucia" Pillson who played the judge), who also took the relatively minor role of the innkeeper.' I didn't think it was that minor," Georgie complained.

"Read on."

"'The language was forceful and conveyed the emotions of the actors to the audience most effectively. Though we might query the accuracy of some of the nautical terms employed...' Oh dear."

"Not to worry. Keep reading."

"'...the overall effect was one of competent professionalism.' Well!" said Georgie. He paused. "But I don't see anything about you anywhere in any of the newspapers."

"That's because I asked them not to mention me. I didn't do this for money. I started doing this as a favour to Irene, and then it became something I was doing as a favour to Tilling. It wasn't for myself at all."

"But there is one thing," said Georgie. "The other evening, you said that there was an enormous joke, but you would only tell us after the performance."

"So there was, and so I did," said Quentin. "Now tell me, how do you think that Elizabeth Mapp-Flint has been behaving, compared to what you were expecting – or perhaps I should say 'fearing'?"

"It's been a very pleasant surprise," Georgie admitted. "There have been little bursts of jealousy, and a little bit of grumbling, but nothing like I expected from her. When I think how things have been in the past sometimes... I have to admire your lion-taming act, as you once described it to us. What is your secret?"

"Stick and carrot, as I said."

"Lions don't eat carrots. And I'm sure if you hit them with a stick they'd just turn round and bite your head off."

"It's a metaphor," said Irene, who had just walked into the room. "Of course Quentin wouldn't dream of offering a carrot to a lion. Or to Mapp, either, come to that."

"What could you offer her as a carrot, then?" Georgie asked Quentin.

"A good part in the pageant, and encouragement for her performance. And it really did turn out that she could be quite good, with or without the underwear."

"I know," said Georgie. "I've never seen that side of her before. I mean the sense of humour, not the undergarments, of course." He blushed.

"She loves to be the centre of attention," Irene said, "but she usually manages that by being nasty to people and being horrid to everyone."

"We all like to be the centre of attention," said Quentin. "It's only actors who are really honest about it."

"Well, you certainly brought out another way for her to show off and be noticed," Georgie said. And do you know, I think she actually enjoyed not being so mean and unpleasant. Even Diva seemed to be quite happy to talk to her. I wonder how long it will last."

"Perhaps for a long time," said Quentin. "Of course, you know what the stick was?"

"The fear of being discovered with contraband?"

"Of course it was. But let me tell you a secret. You are not to tell anyone, Irene, or you Georgie, what I am about to tell you now."

"Not even Lucia?" asked Georgie.

"Especially not Lucia," said Quentin. "It would spoil everything if she were to find out. I have a lawyer friend in London, and I asked him, with no names mentioned or anything, what was the legal position of anyone who found a hoard of what appeared to be contraband from over a hundred years ago, including, for example, silk, or brandy."

"Prison?" suggested Georgie.

"More likely they'd have to pay duty on it," said Irene. "And give it up."

"The answer, my dear friends, is nothing. First, there is no proof that the silk which Elizabeth used to make her dress or the brandy that Major Benjy enjoyed was smuggled and duty was not paid. Secondly, we do not know when it was brought into the country, and therefore what the duty should be. Thirdly, there is a statute of limitations on these things, which almost certainly applies in this case. And lastly, though these are clearly valuable items, they don't count as treasure trove, and the Crown has no right to them. So it's finders keepers. Mapp can keep her dress, and the Major can keep his brandy, either to drink, or to sell for whatever price he can get for it. Alternatively, he can give it to his friends, which is what he did with one cask of the brandy when I told him last night that he had no need to worry about the Customs men."

"Did he really?" asked Georgie. "That seems like a change from his usual self."

"Tell us all about it, Quentin," Irene begged.

"Well, I went round to Grebe, and I got him alone in his study without Elizabeth there."

"Very wise," commented Georgie.

"So I told him what I just told you, and he almost exploded. 'What the deuce do you mean telling me just now?' he said." Quentin's imitation of Major Benjy was almost perfect, and Georgie started to giggle. "I explained that as someone who believed himself to be a smuggler, he would play the part of a smuggler better on stage than a man who was innocent."

"Do you really think so?" asked Georgie.

"Of course not. But he seemed to believe it. Anyway, after a bit, when it had sunk in that the brandy actually was his, and all the silk was Elizabeth's, even though he did tell me that there wasn't that much of the silk that was fit to use, I have never seen a man look so relieved. It was as if he had suddenly become ten years younger. And he told me all about how he came across the brandy. All to do with a sailor friend of his, a Captain Puffin, who had discovered this hoard, and apparently was prepared to share it with Major Benjy if the Major helped dig it up and recover it. But then, apparently, he died of apoplexy or something."

"Captain Puffin," said Irene reflectively. "A little shrimp of a man. With depths so hidden we had no idea they were there at all."

"And that's when he gave you a cask of brandy, after he'd told you all this?"

"Exactly. It's the one we opened earlier together, and I have more than a suspicion that he and Elizabeth have been sampling the contents pretty freely, but there's enough in here for us all to enjoy it. So," and like a magician, he opened a small cabinet to disclose three brandy glasses, which he distributed.

"Your very good health," said Quentin.

"To Quentin Bontemps and all who sail in her," said Georgie, greatly daring.

"And to poor old Dicky Puffin," said Irene.

They drank.

IF YOU ENJOYED THIS STORY...

Please consider writing a review on a Web site such as Amazon or Goodreads.

You may also enjoy some adventures of Sherlock Holmes by Hugh Ashton, who has been described in *The District Messenger*, the newsletter of the Sherlock Holmes Society of London, as being "one of the best writers of new Sherlock Holmes stories, in both plotting and style".

Volumes published so far include :

Tales from the Deed Box of John H. Watson M.D.

More from the Deed Box of John H. Watson M.D.

Secrets from the Deed Box of John H. Watson M.D.

The Darlington Substitution (novel)

Notes from the Dispatch-Box of John H. Watson M.D.

Further Notes from the Dispatch-box of John H. Watson M.D.

The Death of Cardinal Tosca (novel)

The Last Notes from the Dispatch-box of John H. Watson, M.D.

The Trepoff Murder (ebook only)

1894

Without my Boswell

Some Singular Cases of Mr. Sherlock Holmes

The Lichfield Murder

The Adventure of the Bloody Steps

The Adventure of Vanaprastha (ebook only)

Children's detective stories, with beautiful illustrations by Andy Boerger:

Sherlock Ferret and the Missing Necklace
Sherlock Ferret and The Multiplying Masterpieces
Sherlock Ferret and The Poisoned Pond
Sherlock Ferret and the Phantom Photographer
The Adventures of Sherlock Ferret

Mapp and Lucia stories:

Mapp at Fifty
Mapp's Return
La Lucia
A Tilling New Year

Short stories, thrillers, alternative history, and historical science fiction titles:

Tales of Old Japanese
At the Sharpe End
Balance of Powers
Leo's Luck
Beneath Gray Skies
Red Wheels Turning
Angels Unawares
The Untime & The Untime Revisited
Unknown Quantities
On the Other Side of the Sky

Full details of these and more at :
https://HughAshtonBooks.com

ABOUT THE AUTHOR

Hugh Ashton was born in the United Kingdom, and moved to Japan in 1988, where he lived until his return to the UK in 2016.

He is best known for his Sherlock Holmes stories, which have been hailed as some of the most authentic pastiches on the market, and have received favourable reviews from Sherlockians and non-Sherlockians alike.

He has also published other work in a number of genres, including alternative history, historical science fiction, and thrillers, based in Japan, the USA, and the UK.

He currently lives in the historic city of Lichfield with his wife, Yoshiko.

His ramblings may be found on Facebook, Twitter, and in various other places on the Internet. He may be contacted at: author@HughAshtonBooks.com

9 781912 605781